The Ravenstone

The Secret of Ninham Mountain

DIANE SOLOMON & MARK CAREY

The Ravenstone: The Secret of Ninham Mountain
by Diane Solomon and Mark Carey
Eloquent Rascals Publishing
Hillsborough County, NH, USA

Website: http://www.EloquentRascals.com

First Edition
ISBN: 978-0-9907094-3-5

Acknowledgments

Our thanks go to:

Our focused and enthusiastic "first readers" and proof readers: Marsha Campaniello, Deborah Whitman, Laura Carey, James Davis, Cheryl Prottsman, Ella Carroll, Laurie Seymour, Cheryl Kareff, Thelma Tracey.

To Matthew Kane for the wonderful cover image of mountain and river.

To Sergey Ryzhkov for the incredible image of the raven on the front cover.

We appreciate you!

Dedication

*"Every child is an artist, the problem is staying
an artist when you grow up"* ~ Pablo Picasso

We dedicate this book to everyone who revels in the joy of the creative process, whether it be art, music, writing...

Don't let growing up or growing older rob you of your creativity!

Hold on to your childlike heart.

Prologue

—————◈—————

1892: Ninham Mountain,
near Cold Spring, New York

"Where's the chamber?" Nora asked. "Is it much further?" She walked quietly beside her twin brother, Patrick, through the sparse woods. "We'd better not be gone long or Mom will worry." She stopped and gazed behind her. All she could see was the trail disappearing between towering pines, hemlocks, and maples, and dappled sunlight streaming across the forest floor. She could no longer see their family gathered in the big meadow for the twins' thirteenth birthday party.

Patrick got his bearings and hurried forward. "It's around here somewhere – I swear every time I come up here things have moved. But, I know this is the trail I took last time." He grabbed her hand and led her further down a slight path between the trees. He grinned. "We'll get back in time for cake... Oh, and don't tell Mother and Father about the stone chamber, all right?"

"Why not? Is it a secret?"

"Not a secret, exactly. But, somehow I don't think they'd approve." He scowled. "Father, especially, would view it a waste of my time, I'm sure."

Just then, a dark, swooping shadow overhead startled them. It was a great black bird, which appeared out of nowhere and came to rest ten feet away on a bed of pine needles.

"A raven!" Patrick spoke softly, but his excitement was obvious. "They don't usually come so close to people."

"He's huge." whispered his sister. I'd love to draw him, she thought.

The raven fluffed its feathers and tilted its head. Then it stretched high on its black feet, reached into the air with velvety wings and lifted effortlessly off the ground. Gliding down the trail, the bird was nearly out of sight before the kids could react. They raced after the raven, which led them off onto a smaller trail through a break in the bushes. This new trail, covered with a carpet of soft moss and tiny flowers, soon blossomed into a miniature meadow, at the end of which stood the open doorway of a stone chamber.

"Look!" Nora spotted the raven again. "It led us right to it!" The bird stood near the dark doorway, gazing at the opening with unblinking eyes, cocking its head from side to side. In the sunlight, she could see the black feathers gleaming with an iridescent purple hue.

Giant hewn stones supporting a huge capstone created the chamber opening and to one side of the door stood a single pointed stone pillar. Nora had the impression that, rather than having been built into the hill, the stone chamber had emerged right out of the hill, of its own accord. It looked like it had been there forever.

Nora wondered how large it was, inside. That sounded great; the heat of the sun and the exertion of the hike made the cool dark cavity within very enticing.

Nora asked, "Who made it, do you know? What's it for?"

Patrick shrugged and shook his head. As he started for the door, the raven hopped into the chamber and vanished from view. The kids glanced at each other, then ventured slowly into the chamber after their feathered guide.

It took a minute or two for Nora's eyes to adjust to the dark inside the chamber, after the brightness of the sunshine. Slowly, she could make out the inner surfaces of the stone walls and the rough dirt floor. It was not a large space, perhaps ten or twelve feet deep, but they could stand up. The ceiling was a few feet above their heads.

It was empty. Except for the raven.

"Look!" Nora pointed to the back of the chamber where the raven was pecking and scratching at the hard dirt floor near the wall.

"What's it doing?" Patrick started toward the raven, which shied away from him and in a strange, stilted walk, returned to the chamber doorway. There in the sunlight, it stared at them with one black shiny eye, then spread its wings and lifted into the air. When Patrick turned back to the spot where the bird had been scratching, he knelt down in the dirt. "There's something here... something the raven was pecking!"

Nora nodded. She peered down at something glowing yellowish-red with streaks of black. It protruded ever so slightly out of the earth.

"It's so dark in here." Patrick felt around in the dirt with his hands. "Can you move a little, out of the light?"

As Nora shifted to one side, the sunlight streamed down onto the spot where Patrick was scrabbling and the item glowed even brighter. Reaching into his pocket, Patrick pulled out a penknife.

"This is turning out to be a great birthday present," he said. He managed to dust off the exposed portion of the object and Nora could see it was not the same rough stone as everything else in the chamber, but rather smooth and polished and rounded on the end. "It feels warm – isn't that odd? The earth around it is cool. Can you help? The ground here is as hard as stone."

Looking around, Nora found a small flat rock. Forgetting her good party dress and shoes in her excitement, she fell to her knees and began to scratch on the other side of the stone object. It was caked with dirt and the ancient floor held it tight.

"It's like treasure!" she exclaimed.

Patrick merely grunted in response. He finally scraped enough dirt away to get his fingers all the way around the object. He leaned back, pulling hard and the artifact slipped suddenly out of the ground with a spray of dust and dirt. He fell back, victory on his face, and stared down at his prize.

Nora leaned forward to get a closer look. Made of stone, it was about eight or nine inches long and fit comfortably in her brother's hands. It was smooth, resembling the handle of a cane. There were bird's heads etched into the ends, each end the mirror image of the other

"What a lot of dirt," Nora said. "I wish we had some water. And look at it glow!"

"Come on, let's take it outside where we can see it better."

They moved into the doorway, both so intent on the object in Patrick's hands that neither noticed the raven, now perched atop the capstone directly over the entrance. A still and silent sentinel, it watched their every move.

Patrick brushed the carved stone object back and forth on his shirt and picked at the remaining bits of dirt to expose the carvings. "Look at these indents! Here, feel it… how it fits in your hand."

Nora wrapped her fingers around the smooth, warm stone. It could not have fit her hand better if it had been created just for her. "It fits so perfectly. What do you think it's for?"

"No idea," Patrick replied. "But, it's beautiful and looks very old. Kind of looks lit from within, somehow, you know what I mean?" He touched it with the tips of his fingers, feeling the grooves and carvings. "How I'd love to know where this came from... and who created it. Indians? Ancient Romans or Celts? Druids?" He paused. "Sometimes I think I was born in the wrong time."

Nora gave a small smile. "It must have been a magical time, for someone to create something so beautiful."

Patrick seemed mesmerized by the carved icon. "How I wish I were there, where this was made." As he spoke, he slowly reached out to grasp the end that Nora was extending in his direction. His fingers slipped into the contours and wrapped around it almost as if he were reaching for Nora's hand in a handshake. Their thumbs touched.

A bolt of electricity ran through Nora and she shivered.

"What on earth?" Patrick cried out.

The sensation intensified and Nora's every sense began to tremble as if they were in a new and strange dimension. Patrick reached for her arm with his free hand and she grabbed for him at the same moment.

A huge golden arc swept up before them, incorporating everything around them into its vast space. Her ears filled with an overwhelming roaring noise. Then the cave, the doorway, and the sunlit forest all dissolved away as even the ground fell away from their feet. She felt suspended in that golden archway of light with complete utter darkness all around them. The light shimmered and pulsed and began to expand away from them in a long undulating path. She could feel it pulling, reaching for her, beckoning to her.

Patrick leaned into the light, then he stepped forward toward the brilliant shining path, drawing Nora with him. Nora sensed her brother's eagerness, but she did not share it. No, her immediate and total reaction was one of fear and panic. This couldn't be right – no, it felt completely *wrong!*

She shook, she trembled, she felt as if she'd been struck. Then she could not breathe, the air was sucked out of her lungs. In the throes of her terror, she knew, with every cell of her being, that this light held only danger and disaster, that she must run the other direction as fast and hard as she could. With a huge effort that demanded all her will, she pulled herself back. She pulled back with all her might, hoping to save Patrick too. She fell backward, hard, onto the ground, still clutching the stone icon, but Patrick had already let go.

"Patrick!" Nora screamed, scrambling up to her feet and reaching out toward him. He was already out of reach and slipping further and further away. It seemed he was fading, as the golden light drew him further along the shimmering pathway.

As she stood clutching the icon to her chest, unaware of the tears coursing down her cheeks, the raven lifted from its perch on the capstone and flew straight into the light after Patrick.

Then it was gone. The light was gone. And her beloved twin brother was gone. There was nothing but the soft breeze, the quiet, sunlit opening in the forest, and the chamber door behind her. All was as it was before.

Except now, she was alone.

———————————— ❧ ————————————

Chapter 1

———◈———

June 16, 2016, Cold Spring, New York

"You feel invisible," Nadia said in a matter-of-fact tone.

"Yeah, that pretty much sums it up." Her twin brother Aidan kicked at a rock on the sidewalk, sending it skittering across the pavement. "The only A in the whole class for my Wappinger Tribe paper and he didn't say a single word about it."

"I know Dad has a lot on his mind right now– "

Aidan cut her off mid-sentence, "He's always had a lot on his mind, but he used to be so proud of me. Now he doesn't even seem to notice anything I do."

"I don't think it's that simple, Aidan. I know Mom is worried about something, about Dad, I think. I'm just not sure what it is yet."

Aidan muttered, "She always fusses over the genius scientist. How is this any different?" He stopped suddenly in his tracks and grabbed her arm. "Oh, no. You don't think they're getting divorced, do you?"

"No, no, that's not it, it doesn't feel like that." Nadia started walking again. "I can't quite put my finger on it... but it feels big. And not in a good way."

As they turned the corner to their own road, Nadia shook off the bad vibes and the nagging worry that had been haunting her. Beautifully tended historic homes lined both sides of this pretty village street. Nadia waved and shouted hello to Mrs. Hanley, who was in her front garden admiring the pink peonies the size of dinner plates. She loved this walk home, where she caught up with her brother's day and decompressed from school.

Her own home filled her with happiness every time she saw it. It was the only house she had ever lived in and she'd heard stories her entire life about her grandmother, who grew up in this house. Built in 1845, it seemed to hold all of her connection to the past, present and future, her memories, her life and loves. White, with black shutters on the windows, it nestled in a garden of rhododendrons and azaleas, with a wide lawn and blueberry hedge separating it from the road. A deep porch wrapped around the front and side, where Nadia loved to park herself in one of the big wicker chairs and gaze at the meadow-like lawn, with its fruit trees. If she sat very still in the spring, she often saw tiny fawns gamboling around in the wildflowers. Down near the stream separating their property from their neighbor's, she loved to catch the tiny toads she had named "micro-toads." And, her dad had built the kids an awesome tree house in the huge black walnut tree in the back yard. The twins' friends always loved to come to their house.

As the kids ran up the porch stairs, an enormous Maine Coon cat lifted his head to greet them, from his favorite wicker chair. He stretched, arched his back, then plopped his front paws down on the floor of the porch while his hindquarters remained on the chair.

"Hey Nicky, had another hard day, didn't you? Huh, kitty?" Aidan chuckled and reached out to the cat, who answered with a soft "Mmmrrraaa." Nicky wandered over and was rewarded with an ear rub from Aidan.

Nadia fished out her keys from her backpack. "Mom said she'd be back about five and asked that we get started in the attic when we got home. The 'Big Brother, Big Sister' truck is coming tomorrow and Mom said she wants to clear some of that stuff up there." Nadia sighed.

Aidan headed for the kitchen. "First things first. I'm starving. My stomach thinks my throat's been cut."

Nadia laughed. He could always make her laugh. "I'll head up – can you bring me one of those blueberry muffins? Oh, and bring some black garbage bags." She took the stairs two at a time.

The huge attic was three flights up, above the second floor, reached by a steep staircase at the end of the hallway. Her mom and dad dreamed of converting the attic into a media room, office, or playroom. But, she and Aidan liked it just fine the way it was and had played up there since they were little kids. Putting on plays was a favorite pastime and the trunks full of clothes from many generations was like having their own Hollywood wardrobe department. One wall consisted of endless shelves of books and boxes crammed full of even more books were stacked nearby. A trunk full of games and toys that no one had looked at in years sat open on one side of the vaulted space.

Then there were the odd miscellaneous items no one could manage to toss: an ancient rocking horse, a dressmaker's dummy, an ornate headboard, an old painting or two, some tired old braided rugs. All gathering dust and awaiting their fate.

"Why don't we just rent a big dumpster?" Aidan spoke through a mouthful of peanut butter, so it came out a bit garbled.

"That kind of destroys the point of giving stuff away to people who could use it, don't you think?"

Aidan handed her a muffin and looked around. "Yeah. But, honestly, this house has been in the family for over a hundred years, why does Mom want it sorted out *today*?"

Twirling her long dark hair, Nadia clipped it up on top of her head, then dropped to her knees in front of another old trunk. "Some of my favorite books are here." She dug around. "I just found *A Wrinkle in Time.* That goes in the keep pile."

The twins sat down in the shaft of sunlight from the window. As they ate, the quiet was broken by a sudden, raspy, cawing sound.

"That's not from the window – that sounded like it came from in here! Is there a bird trapped up here?" Nadia hopped up to investigate.

"Better make sure the door is shut to the stairs, or Nicky will eat it."

They heard it again. "Graa, graa."

Nadia followed the sound, which took her to the far corner of the attic, where an antique cheval mirror stood. Its glass was smoky with dust and the silver backing so oxidized that her reflection always looked like an old tintype photograph. She looked around for the bird, but a subtle movement in the mirror caught her eye. Was Aidan behind her? No, he was still sitting by the window licking the last of his sandwich off his fingers. She whirled back to the mirror. Just as she began to wipe the dust off the glass with her hand, she jerked back and gasped.

"Uh... Aidan. *Aidan*, get over here... *quick*."

The tone of her voice had him up in a flash and hurrying to join her.

"What is it? What's going on?" He focused on the mirror.

Nadia's eyes were huge as she gaped at the old mirror. There, in the glass, was the shimmering image of what appeared to be a very old man. Wizard-like, he was tall and lean with a long, gray beard. A spark of light reflected from his eyes but she could not make out his features. A deep hood, topping the long brown robe he wore tied at the waist, cast a shadow across his face. He held a gnarled wooden staff in one hand and a large black bird was perched on his shoulder. Suddenly the old man moved! He raised one hand, palm outward and reached slowly toward them.

The kids tripped over each other as they pulled back away from the incredible sight.

"Geez, Aidan, what on earth? Who... what is that? Is this a trick? Is there a camera in here?"

In the mirror, the old man and the raven shimmered in and out of focus like a rippling reflection in a pond, and then they both vanished. Aidan and Nadia were frozen, staring and blinking in disbelief at the dusty old mirror.

Then, they heard the back door slam and their heads snapped in the direction of the sound.

"Hey, Aidan, Nadia, I'm home. Where are you?"

It was their mother's voice and she was heading up the stairs.

They looked quickly back at the mirror but all they saw were their own reflections. But, in front of the mirror, a single black feather appeared before their eyes. For an instant, it hung suspended in the air, then floated gently down to rest on the dusty wooden floorboards at their feet.

Chapter 2

———◈———

"Up here, Mom." It came out as something of a croak, so Aidan cleared his throat and tried again. "We're in the attic."

Genevieve Shaw appeared halfway up the attic stairs. She stopped and peered through the railings.

"Hey, guys. How are you getting on up here? Huh, you both look like the cat that ate the canary. What are you two up to?"

"Uh, nothin', Mom." Nadia gave a bright smile. "We've been sorting through books."

"Good, that's great. But, can you come down and help get dinner going? Heather's making a salad; I need you to set the table. I had a client run late... Dear me, what a list of health problems she has. Oh, and your dad will be home early tonight." She turned back down the stairs.

"Ok, be right there." Then Aidan added, under his breath, "Dad home early? That's a first." He turned back to see Nadia still staring at the mirror. "Good save, Nadia, fast thinking."

She still looked stunned. "Aidan, what on earth was that? Please tell me I'm not crazy... that I didn't imagine that. You saw it too... right? Aidan?" She turned to see if he was paying attention. She hated it when he didn't answer her. "You saw the old man in the robe and the big bird, *right*?"

Aidan nodded, his face serious. Nadia knew he was more intrigued than scared. In his usual analytical way, he was thinking, hard. She watched as he studied the front and back of the mirror and all around it on the unfinished walls and rafters. "I don't see anything anywhere up here that could have created that image. And it couldn't have been a hologram, anyway..."

"Because a hologram doesn't move like that?"

"Because a hologram doesn't drop real feathers. And there is no projector – we'd have seen the beam of light." Aidan reached up to feel all around the top of the mirror and down its sides. "Plus, this is a mirror, not a screen... you can't project an image *into* a mirror."

"What are you looking for?"

He stepped back from the mirror and shrugged. "No idea... I just can't figure it out and it's going to bug me. Why would someone go through this trouble just to mess with us?" He looked around at the rough walls of the unfinished attic, then called out, "Hey, whoever is videoing us, you better not post it online anywhere!"

Nadia slowly shook her head. "What if it's real, Aidan? What if there is an old wizard trying to tell us something? Wouldn't that be the coolest thing?"

Aidan rolled his eyes and shot her a you've-got-to-be-kidding look.

They stood quietly, mystified.

"I wonder if it will happen again..." Aidan gave her a devilish grin.

"Aidan, Nadia!" Their mom's voice held that dreaded I'm-not-going-to-say-it-again tone. The kids hurried down the stairs.

In the kitchen, their older sister Heather was chopping up Romaine lettuce and the twins grabbed silverware and set the table. The kitchen was full of soft early-evening light and good smells emanated from the big sauté pan where onions sizzled gently in olive oil. Nadia's mouth began to water.

The mudroom door opened and their dad, Dr. Michael Shaw, came in, lugging his bulging briefcase in one hand and a big bag of files in the other, which thumped against the doorframe as he entered the kitchen.

"Hi Gen, hi kids." His voice sounded tired. He disappeared into his study, a big butler's pantry that had been co-opted and transformed into a compact but comfortable home office. They heard him sigh and the bag of files hit the floor.

She might not admit this to her girlfriends, but Nadia actually loved the ritual of their family dinner, with everyone around the table once a day. Normally, Nadia would regale them with tales of happenings at school or after school events. Even something as ordinary as a trip to the mall was an excuse to entertain and she knew how, instinctively, to recount it all in great detail and with considerable animation. She loved that she could get everyone laughing.

Tonight dinner was less lively than usual. This was often a time when everyone talked at once, but tonight Heather did most of the talking, seemingly oblivious of the undercurrent of preoccupation at the table. Her best friend Judith (although she insisted on being called "Judessa") had dyed her hair... yet again.

"I wonder if it will all fall out this time." Heather laughed.

Even Nicky was there, lurking quietly under Aidan's chair, hoping for a covert handout. For a cat, he wasn't picky; he even ate cheese. But, Nicky was out of luck tonight. Aidan was clearly distracted and Nadia knew he was still trying to think of a logical explanation for what happened in the attic.

She wondered why her mom was quieter than usual. And her father was in what had become his new default mood: distant and preoccupied.

Heather got up and grabbed her favorite creamy ranch salad dressing from the fridge. "Dad, you want some?" Her father did not even look up. "Hey, Dad, you OK?"

"Not really, sweetheart." Michael spoke for the first time since he walked in the door, except for "Thanks," and "Pass the salt." "I've been waiting for weeks for the final results from the latest compound we've been working on. They finally came through today and they're no better than any of the dead ends we've worked on for the last year. It just seems like there isn't anything new out there anymore. Wondering what this means for the Project."

"What do you mean?" Nadia chimed in between mouthfuls of her favorite garlic mashed potatoes. "I thought people sent you dirt and bits of plants from all over the world."

Her dad's smile brought his tired face to life. "They still do, honey, but it's not like the old days. We used to open those packages feeling pretty confident that we'd find something in them we've never seen before, something with potential. But, I honestly can't remember the last time we cultured anything that we haven't seen 100 times before."

"You mean there's no diversity in plant life anymore?" It was Aidan's turn. "Or less, anyway. We learned about that this year in biology. Hundreds of species are going extinct every year."

"That's right, Aidan." Michael had shifted to soapbox mode. "The planet has become a very small place. There's hardly a square foot of it that someone hasn't stepped on."

Their father had been so distant lately it was good to hear him talk about the Project again, with a bit of passion. "The Project," as their dad always called it, had run like background music for their entire lives. It was practically part of the family. From the moment Nadia was old enough to understand, she'd heard the stories about Grandma Catherine, how she had died of some mysterious disease no one had ever seen before. She knew how important this was to her dad, that he had built a career focused on a cure for this deadly bug.

"We don't seem to have learned any lessons from the mistakes of our past. We dump garbage in the ocean with little or no concern for the creatures that have to live there." Michael was on a roll. "We pump pollution into the air, we cut down incredibly lush diverse rain forests to plant corn to feed cattle."

Michael realized that he had launched into his favorite rant. He smiled at his family and put the fork he'd been driving his points home with down on his plate.

Gen started clearing the table. "You guys are finished with exams, right?"

Aidan grinned and sang out, "Yup, Free-du-um!"

Heather shook her head. "Geez. Lucky you. I still have a humongous physics final. Why on earth did I take *physics?*" Her mom started to speak, but Heather cut her off. "I know, I know, the whole become-a-doctor thing."

Her mom chuckled. "Yes, there is that."

Heather turned toward the door. "Ok, gang, I am off to Carrie's – she and Judith and I are cramming. Bye, all." She gave a wave and headed out.

Her mom gave a little wave to her daughter's retreating back. "See you later honey, don't be too late." As Heather took off, she turned to the twins. "What about you, Nadia? What's left for you – exams and all that?"

"A PILE," Nadia said with a groan. "Does that get me out of dishes?"

Her mom put her hands on her hips in mock outrage.

"Ok, I lied," Nadia admitted. "I'm done. That biology exam today was the last. Phew. I think I did well."

"Honey, you've been applying yourself much better this year. Well done. We're proud of you." Gen turned back to the sink and leaned down for the dish detergent. She suddenly turned back to the twins. "Oh, I nearly forgot. There's a book reading and signing at the bookstore Saturday afternoon – Grandma Liz thought you guys might want to be there. You know, that woman who wrote *The Power of Twins*."

"Sounds good." Aidan juggled a pile of plates and silverware over to the counter. "Uh, Mom, I think I'll work some more on those books in the attic tonight... Want to help, Nadia?"

"Sure!" Nadia popped the last plates in the dishwasher.

Their mom said, "That's great, you two. Thank you." She gave them a skeptical look. "Never thought it would be that much fun working in the attic... "

The kids just grinned at her and headed up the stairs.

Up in the attic, Nadia was drawn, as if by a magnet, to the old mirror. Aidan, hard on her heels, first checked that no one was following them, then closed the attic door at the bottom of the stairs. Joining his sister near the cheval mirror, he reached into an old trunk and yanked out an old torn T-shirt long since relegated to rag duty. He started wiping the mirror. Decades-old dust swept away easily, but his reflection was little improved. The silvering on the back of the glass was tarnished and flaking and was, after all, the reason the mirror was in the attic and not downstairs in use.

Nadia said, "Hmmm. Poor old mirror has certainly seen better days, hasn't it?"

"Yeah, it's a real mess. This helps a bit, though, look at that. I just took it from piece of junk to plenty good enough. Just wanted to get a better look at it."

Nadia caught herself gnawing on her thumbnail and yanked it out of her mouth. She'd been working hard to stop the nervous chewing of her nails and cuticles and was hard on herself when she caught herself backsliding.

Aidan was still studying the old mirror. "You know, there's no way someone could have rigged this mirror without disturbing all that dust."

The twins stared at each other for a moment, then back at the dingy glass.

Nadia shrugged. "Well, I just can't believe it happened. Did we take a nap up here or something and dream it?"

Suddenly, they both drew in a sharp breath. The image in the mirror was distorting and flexing. It looked like the ripples from a pebble tossed in a pond, but in reverse. Concentric rings converged in the center and the ripples got smaller and smaller until an image slowly came into focus. It was the same old man, who seemed suspended in a dusky gray cloud, like smoke, which billowed all around him.

"Oh, *Aidan*." Nadia gasped and stepped closer to her brother. "It's happening again..."

As she grabbed her brother's hand, the image intensified and sharpened into focus. The old man raised his hand and pointed toward them with his index finger. Then he began to slowly move his finger in little swirling motions as if he were writing in the air. The kids were rooted to the spot, hardly breathing. Through the smoky mist, they could see writing, of some sort, appear in front of the old man. It seemed to drift through a cloud and settle on the inner surface of the mirror's glass, where it slowly came into focus.

"What does it say?" Nadia asked. "It doesn't mean a thing to me... it doesn't even look like our alphabet."

When the old man lowered his arm, the writing continued to appear for a few moments, as if it had a very long way to travel. He stood still, as if waiting. Watching them.

Nadia dropped her brother's hand, looking quickly around. "We need something to write with. Quick – I know you have a photographic memory, but we have to write that down, somehow!"

The image of the old man began to dissolve, leaving only the cryptic message behind. Then it, too, slowly started to wane, in the undulating smoke, threatening to become nothing but a memory.

Quick as a flash, Aidan reached into his pocket for his cell phone and grabbed a couple of shots of the mirror with its strange, unintelligible writing.

"Wait, sir, please come back. Tell us what this means. We can't read it!" But, Nadia's pleas hung in the still attic air. The old man and the writing were gone. What was, an instant ago, a window to another world was again just a shabby old mirror.

As the twins stood staring at their own shocked reflections, they could ever so slightly detect the faint smell of smoke.

———————◈———————

Chapter 3

———❋———

"Where's my backpack? Hang on... forgot something." Aidan ran back up the porch steps into the house. When he reappeared, he was folding an 8 x 10 piece of white paper in half, then quarters, and jamming it into his jean's pocket.

The kids headed off in the direction of town.

"I know we agreed that we can't even tell Grandma Liz," said Aidan. "But, I thought about it all day. I know she might be able to help, somehow. I want to ask her about the weird writing, but I don't want the rest of the world to see it."

Nadia stopped up short. "You didn't print out the picture did you? We can't show her that!"

"I know, I'm not an idiot. I traced it." Aidan had not stopped when she had and now she hurried to catch up.

"How'd you do that?"

"I printed out the jpg, large, and then traced it onto a piece of printer paper."

"Wow, cool," Nadia said and grinned. Her brother always impressed her. She often said, "Aidan knows a lot of stuff about a lot of stuff." And she wondered how he did.

The twins continued the half-mile or so to Corvid Books. Their Grandmother's bookstore stood proudly on historic Main Street in the village of Cold Spring, New York, a small community on the Hudson River, about an hour north of New York City. Famous in the 19th century for West Point Foundry and arms manufacturing, it was now a quaint little town full of antique shops, galleries, ice cream parlors and cafes. Although the town was often heaving with tourists in the summer, that night, at 5 o'clock on a Friday in June, the street was peaceful.

As they neared the front door of the bookstore, Aidan was still musing. "We can't let anyone else know about this. It has to be our secret."

"Absolutely," Nadia agreed. "Because if it is *real*–"

Aidan tried to jump in. "But–"

"Hang on, hang on," Nadia said. "If it *is* real, the grown-ups will take over and they'll cut us out of it completely. They'll probably even take the mirror away."

Aidan gave a nod of agreement. "And if it's *not* real and someone is jerking us around – which seems pretty likely at this point – we'll end up looking like fools."

He pushed open the heavy wooden door to the bookstore and the old brass bell attached to the top announced their arrival. Nadia waited while he held the door open for two women, laden with shopping bags, as they left the shop. She glanced up at the big sign over the door, with the carved black bird under the title, Corvid Books.

"Look, it's a crow's head. I never really noticed before."

"That's a raven," Aidan said. "All the birds that are similar to ravens like crows and jays are called Corvids, but the raven is the biggest of them all. They're very smart, kind of the King of the Corvids."

Once again, not surprised that Aidan knew weird stuff, Nadia just raised an eyebrow.

Aidan continued, "Grandma Liz told me she named the store "Corvid Books" after the raven. She said the raven, in Celtic mythology, was the shape-shifter, and a guide in supernatural events. When I looked it up online it said, 'Expect magic.'"

Nadia stepped closer to Aidan and asked, softly, "And the bird we saw in the mirror?"

"That was a raven, too."

"So cool," she breathed.

Crossing the threshold of Corvid Books, it always felt to Nadia that she was stepping back in time. As if you might see Washington Irving himself, reading to kids from *Rip Van Winkle,* in a big overstuffed chair under a window. The creaky pine floorboards had gaps between them and the building itself smelled a little of dust and mildew and old paper. All the previous owners of this shop had resisted updating it for at least the last hundred years. Hardwood bookcases lined the walls. Their arched tops and frieze moldings lent an old-world look and feel and the shelves were so ancient they were worn smooth in the middle. The bookstore was a maze of different levels and spaces; turning a corner, through an arched doorway, yet another nook appeared. Up a step here, down a ramp there, every trip to Corvid Books was an adventure.

She spotted her grandmother, talking with a woman in the Yoga and Meditation section and started toward her. It was hard to miss Grandma Liz, she always stood out, in her vibrant clothes and jewelry. Today, she was all in turquoise and black, with huge silver and turquoise jewelry, in the southwest American Indian style. With her long skirts and piles of silver arm bangles, she managed to look glamorous and yet like an aging hippy at the same time, Nadia thought. A glamorous hippy. Perfect! But, it was more than her clothes and jewelry. Grandma Liz sort of filled the room, somehow. What her dad called a big personality. Nadia smiled to herself. She sure is that, she thought.

As the customer turned away, Liz spotted the twins approaching. "Hey! How are my favorite twins?"

Aidan grinned – this was a ritual. "I bet you say that to all the twins."

She hugged them warmly. "Not a chance, buddy. This is a nice surprise – I didn't think I was seeing you till *The Power of Twins* book-reading. You're coming, right?"

"Sure are, Aunty-Gran, sounds fun," Nadia said. "But, we came by today because we need your help with something."

"'Aunty-Gran.' My, I haven't heard that in a while! OK, what can I help you with?"

Aidan hesitated. "Can we go up to your office?"

They trudged up the winding stairs, only having to stop twice while Grandma Liz talked with someone. A record, Nadia thought. The rest of the way, she chatted merrily, about the upcoming author visit.

"You guys will love the book – the author has twins in her family, too. But, I *know* she doesn't have as many twins as we do. Does anyone?" Liz chuckled.

There really were an unusual number of twins in their family tree. The Discovery Channel had even approached them for an interview about their family. They had hinted about including them in an upcoming documentary special on twins.

In her office, their grandmother plopped down in the big leather chair behind her cluttered desk. "Ok, here we are… shoot. What's up?"

Aidan pulled the folded piece of paper, now pretty crumpled, out of his jeans pocket, and handed it to her. "Do you have any idea what language this is? We've never seen anything like it. Figured you might know…"

Liz glanced at the paper only briefly before flipping it over and spreading it smooth on the top of her desk. "It's reversed. It's a mirror image."

The kids shot each other a look.

Liz then held it up to the light for them. "See? Look at it from the back, through the paper."

"Ooh, what's it say?" Nadia peered closely at the writing and tried to read it aloud. "Breeth-noo."

```
breathnú

ar an

scáthán
```

"I think it is "Bre-ath-noo." Liz got up and strolled over to a bookcase on one wall and ran her finger along some big reference books until she found the one she wanted. "It's Irish, I'm sure of that, but don't know what 'breathnu' means."Scathan' is 'looking glass,' or 'mirror,' as I recall."

The kids shot each other another look, which Liz caught out of the corner of her eye.

"Where did this come from?" Liz juggled the large book over to her desk and sat down to take a closer look.

Aidan's voice was nonchalant. "Oh, it's just something we found online when we were looking up Irish myths and legends."

"Ah, here we are, I found it. 'Breathnu.' It means 'observation.' Hang on, as a verb it's 'Look at.'" She thumbed through more pages. "Hmmm, and since 'scathan' is 'looking glass' or mirror, I think the whole phrase means 'Look in the mirror.'" She looked back and forth at the twins and smiled. "Does that help? Do you need it for something?"

"No not really," Aidan said quickly. "It just bugged us that we couldn't figure it out and we knew you could help. Thanks, Aunty-Gran."

Liz gave them a thoughtful look. "I wonder what you kids are up to. Now, don't try to look innocent, it doesn't fly with me." She smiled. "Sometimes I wish I could read everyone's mind, like you do, Nadia."

"Everyone's but yours, Aunty-Gran." She smiled back as she hugged her grandmother.

Liz waved them off, wrist bangles jangling. "Great to see you, but I have to get back downstairs."

"Thanks, Aunty-Gran. See you Saturday." Aidan grabbed the paper, stuffed it back in his pocket and the kids took off back down the stairs.

"Look in the mirror, seriously?" Nadia mocked. "What kind of a stupid message is that? We *were* looking in the mirror. I don't think he's a wizard, I think he's an idiot." She yanked the shop door open and headed out to the sidewalk.

"I need some time to *think*." Aidan's face was scrunched up with concentration. Nadia knew he'd drive himself crazy working on it. She didn't have as much patience – her mom told her so all the time. She sighed. Come on, Nadia, she thought, we're missing something.

The twins headed home, silent for a block or two.

"You know, I used to think I couldn't read Grandma Liz because there was nothing to read." Nadia spoke slowly, searching for how to put her thoughts into words for her brother. "You know what I mean, like she was an open book, no secrets. But... I'm starting to think I might have been wrong about that. When I try to reach her on that level,

nothing happens. It's not like I get through and I don't find anything, it's like I just can't get through. Like there is a block or a wall." She looked over at him. "Do you get anything from her? Do you ever try anymore?"

"Nah. You know I don't have your gift."

"You used to, Aidan."

"Yeah, but only with you. I never could read other people." Aidan shrugged. "It might have just been coincidence, anyway."

Nadia knew he accepted her reading people because he loved and respected her. But, he really thinks it's hokum, she thought. And Dad played it down and often joked with Aidan about it. It used to hurt her feelings, but she was used to it, now and besides, eventually they would see that she was right!

Dad said something else that was cool, she remembered. He said between Aidan and Nadia, they were one whole brain: Aidan's was the scientific side and Nadia's the intuitive side. Grandma Liz, however, explained it differently. And she was quite serious. She always said she and Aidan were synergistic, or "greater than the sum of the parts." When Aidan asked her what that meant, she replied, "You are one. Nadia is one. Together you are three."

Something about that felt right to Nadia. They were very close and understood each other, often without even speaking. Be that as it may, she and her twin brother were different in many ways. They looked different, thought differently, behaved differently. She had fine dark brown hair and deep blue eyes while he had thick wavy light brown hair and brown eyes. She was intuitive; he was rational, logical. She was impulsive, he thought things out first. As for this whole strange event in the mirror, Nadia was ready to believe that magic had happened. She hoped it had! Not her brother; she knew it would be very hard for him to accept.

Nadia said softly, "Hmmm... Look in the mirror."

Aidan was quieter than usual for the rest of the way home. "What are we missing?" he muttered.

Nadia tossed it around in her mind. Oh, she was so disappointed. On the way to see Grandma Liz, her expectations had been so high. She had no idea what the writing meant but had hoped it would be a clue that would lead them to the next step in this mystery. Instead, what they found out seemed like no help at all. In fact, it seemed deliberately pointless.

Aidan muttered, "I hope this isn't an elaborate hoax that'll come crashing down around us." He paused, looking thoughtful. "But you know, there's something really nagging at me. The more I try to pin it down the more it is gone."

"Well, you know what Mom always says. Don't work at it, think about something else and it'll come clear."

As they climbed the porch steps to the house, Aidan said over his shoulder, "Meet me in the attic when everyone's gone to bed. We have to figure this out."

Chapter 4

———◆———

The twins stood facing the old cheval mirror.

"Well, I looked up those words, myself, after we got home and Aunty-Gran is right – about what each word means, anyway. But, maybe there is more than one way to look at the whole phrase... I can't wrap my head around it yet. Could there be some other meaning?" Aidan had used translation sites online and "Breathnu ar an scathan" was definitely Irish and meant, "Look in the mirror."

Aidan and Nadia had said good night to everyone early, then hung around their rooms, waiting until the house was still. It seemed to take forever, but finally, they saw their parents' bedroom light go out and they tiptoed up to the attic. Aidan held up his cell phone for light and gently stopped Nadia from flicking on the attic light switch. She nodded and gave him a thumbs-up.

Staring into the old mirror again, Nadia whispered, "Ok, so here we are. Looking in the stupid mirror." She chewed on the cuticle of her thumb, then caught herself. She tucked her thumbs inside fists and held them down at her sides, determined not to start that again.

There was a sudden movement in the mirror and the old man began to materialize. He looked haunting and ghostlike in the hard small light from the cell phone. The raven was again perched on his shoulder.

"We don't understand, sir. The words said, 'Look in the mirror.'" Nadia spoke directly to the figure in the glass. "But, we *are* looking in the mirror. What are you trying to tell us?"

"You are in the mirror – is that it?" Aidan asked.

The figure did not reply. As they stared, he slowly raised the long staff in his hand and the raven gently lifted off his shoulder and flew directly toward them. The twins ducked, instinctively, just as the large ebony bird penetrated the plane separating reflection from reality, passing through the mirror, right into the attic itself. It was now physically present and still coming toward them.

Aidan and Nadia tumbled back onto the floor and they could feel the breeze from the bird's wings as it passed over their heads. Aidan's phone skittered across the attic rug and its light went out. As they jumped to their feet and peered around in the darkness, they could make out the raven, standing on a pile of boxes behind them, as real as they were. His jet-black feathers gleamed in the moonlight streaming in through the attic window. Only a small patch of white on his neck broke the shiny black coloring. Nadia looked back at the mirror, but the figure had vanished. The raven, however, remained.

The twins were stunned. Aidan took a step toward Nadia as if to protect her, but Nadia did not feel afraid. She was startled and excited, to be sure, but was more in awe than frightened.

Just as she was wondering what their next move should be, the bird hopped down to the attic floor and waddled, unconcerned, between the two of them to the base of the cheval mirror. The kids shuffled back a bit, eyes wide in wonderment, giving it some space.

The raven began to peck gently at the base of the mirror. Then he turned and looked at them for a moment, before turning once again to continue its pecking.

Aidan spoke softly, "What on earth is he doing now?"

Nadia stared at the bird. "Look how he keeps looking back at us."

She moved carefully toward the mirror, trying not to spook the raven. Aidan positioned himself between his sister and this strange bird. Then he reached for his sister's hand and as his fingers closed around hers, the old man reappeared in the glass as though stepping out of shadow. This time, he took half a step forward and, leaning on the staff with one hand, he pointed with the other down at the iridescent bird at the base of the old mirror.

Letting go of Nadia's hand, Aidan threw his arms up and asked, "What? What do you want us to do?" The figure in the mirror just receded and faded once again.

Aidan and Nadia stood frozen, eyes locked on the raven for a few moments more. It stared directly at them, head tilted to one side as though it had been waiting for them to pay attention, then pecked three measured pecks on the base of the mirror. Turning back to them, it stretched its wings and lifted off the attic floor. Nadia sucked in a breath, but together the twins held their ground. Just as the bird reached eye level, it disintegrated. It gently burst into a shower of glittery particles, evaporating as they drifted down, never reaching the attic floor. Like silent fireworks in the night sky.

Speechless, they stood still while the attic slowly returned to its normal dark dusty condition, as if nothing had ever happened. Then they heard the sound of water running in one of the bathrooms.

"Yikes," Nadia whispered. "What are we going to tell them if they find us up here in the middle of the night?"

"Shhhh. Just hold on, it's probably nothing. We don't know that they heard anything."

They stayed still, waiting for a minute or two. There was silence.

"That was close," Nadia whispered. "They must've gone back to bed."

Aidan quietly picked up his phone and pressed the on button. "Good." He sighed. "It isn't broken. Geez, Mom and Dad would kill me if they had to buy me another one."

Using it as a flashlight, he knelt down to look at the spot where the raven had been pecking. He ran his hands over the smooth wooden base.

"You've been over it and over it and not found anything. Come on, Aidan, we should get out of here." Nadia was starting to get nervous. "I'm afraid Mom and Dad are going to catch us and want to know what we're doing. Come on, tomorrow is Saturday – we can mess around up here all we want during the day. It would be a lot easier to explain."

Downstairs, Aidan flopped down at the kitchen table. However, Nadia couldn't sit. She felt restless, shaken and even though it was June, a bit chilled.

"Want some hot chocolate?" Nadia didn't wait for an answer from her brother; she knew he was miles away, but would drink whatever she put in front of him.

The clank of the saucepan on the stove roused her brother. "That raven was real," Aidan said. "He was *real...* Oh, man." He jumped up and joined Nadia in front of the stove and peered over her shoulder. "What are you doing?"

"Can you grab me the whisk?" Nadia asked, over her shoulder.

"Sure... What's a whisk and where is it?"

Nadia rolled her eyes. "Over there." She pointed toward the big white hutch near the table. "It's in the hutch."

"Oh." Aidan started for the hutch, then suddenly stopped, whirled around, hands up to his forehead, his eyes wide.

"What?" She was watching that the milk didn't boil over and trying to watch Aidan.

"In the mirror... *In* the mirror!" he said. Nadia just looked at him. He was grinning and held out his hands, palms up, as if it was perfectly obvious. "Of course, why didn't I think of that before?" He shot out of the kitchen at a near-run and headed for the stairs.

"Wait for me, where you going, what are you talking about?" Nadia flicked off the burner and raced after him. "Wait," she whispered again. "Will you please stop and talk to me? *What are you doing?"*

Pausing briefly at the top of the stairs, Aidan waved hard for her to be quiet as he listened for any activity from the rest of their sleeping family. Hearing none, he was off again and scurrying toward the attic stairs, with Nadia right behind him. As quickly and quietly as they could, the twins slipped up the last flight of stairs to the attic and stood in the beam of moonlight before the mirror.

"For crying out loud Aidan, will you please tell me what you're doing?" She was breathless and irritated.

"His words were 'Look in the mirror.' It means look *in* the mirror."

"I dare you to say it one more time." Nadia was actually clenching her fist.

"Something has been bugging me, nagging at me, and then it hit me!" Aidan shifted his focus back to the mirror. He squatted down and ran his hands over, around and finally under the wooden base, concentrating his search below the very spot the raven had been pecking.

"In the mirror," he whispered as he felt around the mirror base. "Maybe it doesn't mean looking in the mirror like you usually look in the mirror, maybe it means to look *inside* the physical mirror!"

At that moment, Aidan's searching finger found the cleverly hidden trigger. Nadia heard a soft metallic click and a small drawer, invisible a moment before, popped open about an inch. She dropped down next to her brother, who had already grabbed the front of the drawer with two fingers and was sliding it open.

"There was a button underneath," Aidan said softly. "It felt like the head of a nail but when I pushed it, it moved." He continued to pull the drawer until it was fully open. It was about a foot from side to side and front to back and four inches deep. He used the cell phone once again as a flashlight to get a better look.

The twins stared into the drawer. Inside, on a white satin pillow rested an intricately carved stone object.

"Look!" Nadia breathed.

Aidan reached in and slowly removed the object. It was made of black shiny stone and it was carved so that it looked exactly the same from either end. On each end was an intricate carving of a raven's head with one wing sweeping back.

Nadia touched it gently. "Can I hold it?" Aidan dropped it into Nadia's hand and turned back to the drawer. He removed the pillow, turned it over then back again, and squeezed it here and there to see if there was anything inside it. Then he leaned closer and looked into the drawer itself and ran his hand into the back to feel for anything else. It was empty. The only two things the drawer had contained were the satin pillow in Aidan's hand and the carved stone, in Nadia's.

Nadia was still examining the stone. "Why did he want us to find this? Where did it come from? Who hid it and why did they hide it in this mirror? Wow, it's like finding treasure!"

Aidan nodded, "You're right. This whole thing is really happening, Nadia. It's *real*. Man, this is so freaking cool!'

Nadia's eyes were still glued to the stone object. "You're right, this is so exciting! How do we figure out what it is? Should we ask mom or dad? We don't have to tell them about the mirror, just that we found this up here? Or maybe Grandma Liz knows... Grandma Catherine lived here before us; do you suppose it was hers or Grandpa Art's?"

Aidan was shaking his head slowly. "I want to keep this to ourselves for awhile, OK? It may be valuable, I know, and we might have to tell them eventually, but let's just hang on for awhile."

"Ok. And look," said Nadia. holding the stone out toward her brother, "See how your hand fits around it. Like I'm shaking a hand. Or, like the grip on the handlebars of your bike."

Aidan grasped the stone from the other end. His fingers slid smoothly into the contours and his thumb pressed up against his sister's.

Nadia sighed. "I don't know how I'll sleep tonight."

They were silent for a few moments, each lost in thought as they stared down at the mysterious stone they held between them.

A shock of energy coursed through her and Nadia gasped.

"What the– ?" Aidan cried.

The energy grew and the next instant Nadia saw a giant golden arc appear in front of her, sweeping her into its light. A roaring sound filled her ears and everything around her shimmered and morphed. Suddenly they were sucked along a short gold path of light.

Then, just as quickly as it happened, everything settled and came back into focus. The feeling of electricity in her veins receded and Nadia took a deep breath. She quickly looked around her and was blinded by the bright sunshine streaming in the window. "Wait – what?" she exclaimed.

The twins, shocked, stared around the attic.

"What was that? What on earth's going on?" Hearing voices in the distance, Nadia slipped quietly across the attic floor, down the stairs and as quietly as possible cracked the door to the second-floor hallway. Yes, voices were coming from downstairs, from either the kitchen or family room. She felt her heart beating double time. What was going on? Something *weird*, that's for sure.

Aidan hurried down the steps and pushed in front of her, listening at the door. "Why is everyone up?" he whispered.

They crept into the hallway, then tiptoed to the head of the main stairs. Just then, Heather laughed out loud and they could hear her friend Judith's voice, as well. With Aidan leading, they continued cautiously down the stairs, remembering to walk on the outer edges of the steps so they wouldn't creak. Just as Nadia was considering simply calling out to her family, she and her brother rounded the bend in the stairs and could see down into the kitchen.

Aidan gasped and jumped back, stopping Nadia from stepping out into full view of those in the kitchen. He motioned "shh" to her with a finger to lips and pointed hard at the kitchen.

Nadia gestured, "what?" with a palm toward the ceiling and peeked around to see what had just shocked her brother.

There, sitting at the big wooden table, were Nadia and Aidan, themselves! The twins, on the stairs, were looking at *themselves* sitting at the kitchen table. This was just not possible. Nadia's hand flew up to her mouth and her heart stopped for a moment in her chest. She pulled back hard, so not to be seen. Then she peeked out again, very carefully. No, she did not imagine it; there was Aidan sitting at the table, eating Cheerios. Heather and Judessa were stirring dough in a large yellow pottery bowl and they could hear their mom's bluegrass music playing from the other room. And yes, there *she* was, real as life, eating toast and honey in the kitchen.

She blinked hard, thinking her eyes were playing tricks on her. Maybe she was looking at someone who just looked like her. No such luck – there was no denying that Aidan was sitting right next to her. She felt as if her brain had turned to mush. She couldn't think straight. Fear tore through her and Aidan looked like he was in shock; his hand was gripping hers so tightly it hurt. What on earth was going on?

Aidan pulled Nadia back up the stairs. But, just as they reached the second-floor landing, their mother stepped out of her bedroom and stopped right in front of them.

"Hey you guys, what are you doing back in your PJs? I thought you were already dressed." Still too dumbfounded to speak, Aidan and Nadia just stared and shrugged at their mother. Before they could come up with any sort of answer, the phone in their mom's hand began to buzz.

"Hey Sis, I was just going to call you." There was a pause while she listened. "Hang on a sec, Suze." She turned to the kids. "Great news. Your Aunt Suzanne is fine with leaving Monday for New Hampshire." The twins nodded. Their mom gave them a funny, searching look.

"What's wrong with you two? You look like you've seen a ghost."

Chapter 5

———❖———

The twins raced back up to the attic. Fortunately, their mom had headed down the hallway, intent on her call with her sister, not waiting for a reply from them.

"I feel like I just stepped into a nightmare!" Though safe for the moment in the attic, Nadia did not feel safe at all. "Tell me that didn't just happen." She was on the verge of tears. "Please, Aidan, tell me what's going on."

He took her by the shoulders. "Nadia, keep your voice down. And you have to slow down – you're going to hyperventilate. Please, close your mouth, breathe slowly. It's OK, we are OK." He grabbed his cell phone and stared at it.

"What? You're going to play with your phone, now?" Nadia wanted to shake him.

"I think I know... but it seems so impossible."

"Tell me!"

He cleared his throat. "I'm waiting..." He was still looking down at his phone.

"What? What *for*?"

"I think we traveled through time."

There was a shocked silent moment. Nadia's mouth gaped open again. "What?"

"Shh! Keep it down."

Nadia looked over his shoulder at the iPhone. "What are you looking at?" She could see the date and time, displayed on the screen.

10:14 p.m.   Friday, June 16

As she stared, it suddenly changed.

10:14 a.m.   Saturday, June 17

She blinked. Yes, it said *Saturday,* June 17. "No. *No...* This says it is tomorrow. It's *tomorrow*?"

"Yeah, I think it is. The phone just updated itself."

Nadia sat down abruptly, feeling like she might fall down if she didn't.

"If it is... OK, think about this for a minute. What's Mom going to think when she goes back to the kitchen and there, as big as life, are you and I sitting there, dressed? She's just seen us on the stairs in pajamas..."

"Oh, Aidan, come on. Bigger picture. How do we get *home*? How do we get back to... um... last night?"

"Don't know yet." He studied her face, which she was sure must be white as a sheet. "We'll be OK." But, he didn't look all that confident, she thought.

"So, what are we supposed to do now?" Nadia caught herself speaking too loudly and dropped her voice to a frantic whisper. "Are we stuck here? Do they catch up to us? Do we catch up to them? I don't understand." She finished on a soft wail.

"OK, calm down. We need to be constructive, here. We are fine, Nadia, we're not in any danger. But, it happened when we were holding this stone bird thing. We need to use it, again, somehow and get back to last night."

"But, I don't know how we did it the first time, so how are we supposed to do it again?"

"First, we think it through," Aidan said firmly. He sounded confident and that gave Nadia hope. "We remember everything we did step-by-step."

She reached for the Ravenstone, as she now thought of it and slipped her hand around one end. She held it out and Aidan did the same and as he wrapped his hand around the mysterious stone, their thumbs touched. They looked into each other's eyes, but there was no magic, only silence and tomorrow's sunshine streaming through the attic window.

"What do we do next? What did we do to make this happen?" They stood there in thought, for a few more moments, but then she couldn't stand the suspense. "What happens if we don't do anything, if we just stay here and hide... and get some sleep? Will time eventually just merge back together?"

"I don't know." Aidan shook his head. "What if that doesn't work? There will be two sets of us... Besides, Mom and Dad would wonder where we are in the morning when we aren't in bed. We have to get back!"

"Maybe we should go down and tell Mom what happened." Nadia was trying hard not to cry, but a tear slipped down her cheek.

"And face *ourselves*? I have no idea what that might do – I've never read a manual for time travel – but I am pretty confident that should be one of our last options, not our first. I'm not giving up that easily! We have to try everything we can think of. Come on, let's figure it out. We did it once, we can do it again... Close your eyes and remember."

Aidan said, "Picture last night. Pretend it's last night. Let's see, what were we doing when the time shift happened?"

The kids were still, eyes closed.

"I'm not sure... it happened so suddenly," Nadia whispered.

"I know." There was a silence. Then Aidan spoke again, very softly. "But, now I just want to be back in the right time."

She nodded. I just want to go home to the right time, to my real time, she thought, another tear joining the first on her cheek. I want to go back to last night, June 16, to the correct time. She pictured the moment she first held the Ravenstone.

Suddenly they felt the electricity running through them again and the golden arc appeared. The roaring noise returned. And just like that, it happened. With a shudder and a wave of dizziness, Nadia was drawn through the golden arc of light. She shut her eyes for a moment and when she reopened them, the sunlight that had been cascading across the attic floor was gone. There was no sound. No voices in the kitchen, no birds singing outside the house. Just the two of them, holding the Ravenstone, in the moonlight.

Chapter 6

———◈———

The next morning started early for Nadia. The events of Friday night had left her drained. Finding the Ravenstone, the shocking trip through time to Saturday morning, and the frantic scramble back to "real time" had taken all of the wind out of her sails. She tossed and turned all night and when morning finally came, she felt as if she hadn't slept at all.

To complicate matters, that sense of foreboding was there again. Her sense was that it was different and separate from the stress of travelling through time. She just couldn't put her finger on it and feeling exhausted wasn't helping.

She gave up trying to sleep at about six o'clock when she heard voices. Stepping out into the hall, she could tell they came from her parents' room. Something in the tone of the conversation made her sneak down the hall and listen outside their bedroom. She didn't even stop to consider that eavesdropping was impolite or wrong, because she could sense deep inside this was important and that it concerned her. And Aidan.

She stood very still outside their door. She heard her dad's voice.

"I just can't give it up, Gen. It is my life's work."

"Maybe you've done enough. Maybe someone else could pick up the baton. I know how important the Project is to you, honey, but is it possible it's become... a bit of an obsession?" His wife spoke gently and before he could respond, she asked, "Are you sure it's worth causing such enormous upheaval to the kids' lives?"

"It won't kill them. And they'll understand."

"I don't know about that, Michael. It will be very hard for them."

Nadia's heart started to pound. What would be hard for us? "Upheaval" to our lives? What is Mom talking about? Is this the bad news I've been sensing?

Hearing one of them coming toward the door, she scurried back to her own room, shutting the door quietly behind her.

Later that morning, it felt very weird to be the ones sitting at the table in the kitchen where they had seen themselves last night, from the stairs. It was a bit spooky, even surreal, Nadia thought, as she sat eating breakfast with her brother. Heather wandered in, yawning and made a beeline for the coffee pot. Then Judith (oops, Judessa, thought Nadia) arrived, sporting her new purple hair. Nadia was amazed her mother let her do it. She knew she'd get an earful from her mom if she dyed her hair some weird color. Heather, her own natural ash blonde tresses pulled up in a ponytail, measured out all the ingredients for chocolate chip cookies.

"They're for tomorrow – Aunty-Gran is taking a bunch of us to Ninham Mountain to see a stone chamber," Nadia explained to Judessa. "And have a picnic."

"Sounds fun. But... *'Antigran...'*? What's that?" Judessa asked as she stirred the chocolate chips into the dough in a big mixing bowl.

"Not 'what,' *who.*' 'Aunty Gran.' That's what we call Grandma Liz." Aidan chuckled. "She is our grand aunt and also our grandmother..."

Aidan's brief explanation had not cleared anything up for Judessa, that was for sure, thought Nadia. She grinned. Judessa could do deer-in-the-headlights like she'd invented the look and she was doing it now.

Aidan went on. "You see, Grandma Liz had a twin sister, Catherine. Catherine was our biological grandmother. We never knew her – she died when Dad was 15." He sneaked a lump of cookie dough from the bowl and popped it in his mouth before Heather could swat his hand away. "Anyway, Grandma Catherine was married to Grandpa Art and a few years after she died, Grandpa married Liz. That makes Grandma Liz our grandaunt and our grandmother. So we call her Aunty-Gran."

"Oh." Judessa swept a strand of purple hair off of her face, not realizing she'd left a chunk of cookie dough on the top of her ear.

"There's just no easy way to explain that one," Heather laughed as she wiped the cookie dough off her friend's ear. "But, it is very romantic, don't you think? Grandma Liz had always been in love with Grandpa Art, but he married her twin sister. She didn't marry for years – I wonder if she was pining for grandpa?"

Aidan rolled his eyes.

Heather continued, her eyes dreamy. "But, after Catherine died, Grandpa Art fell in love with Liz... "She looked at Judessa. "Isn't that a great story?"

48

Nadia had remained quiet through this, which was unusual for her. She was preoccupied. She kept hearing, "such enormous upheaval to the kids' lives," over and over again in her head. And lately she was aware of odd, distracted vibes from her mom. She was scared to ask what was going on. Might be best not to know. Plus, she was still trying to process the whole time-travel experience. It all left her feeling off-kilter. She was glad Nicky was on her lap. He rubbed his face against her hand and his warmth and purr were comforting.

Heather chatted with Judith but Nadia wasn't listening anymore. What next with the Ravenstone? She kept reminding herself that it was not a toy and in fact, could be quite dangerous. They had somehow managed to find their way "home," but she wasn't sure how. What if they held the stone again and it whisked them away to some deadly time or place from which they couldn't return?

They had replaced the Ravenstone in the drawer in the mirror before they crept downstairs to bed. Aidan had said it might be best to leave it there. At least for the moment. He was probably right.

Nadia couldn't help but peer at the doorway leading to the stairs from time to time. Would she see herself and Aidan peeking around the wall into the kitchen? Would she hear Mom talking to them on the stairs? Did it work that way?

She had to stop thinking about it or her head would explode. She was sure, if she stopped thinking about it, the answer would just come to her. OK. Best to think about something else. Well, there was the upcoming summer vacation to New Hampshire, to their other Grandmother's house and they would have some fun with their cousins. When her mom came into the kitchen from upstairs, she said, without thinking, "Hey Mom, so cool that Aunt Suzanne can take us up to New Hampshire on Monday. It's always fun with Matt and Ryan."

She muttered a soft, "Ow!" as Aidan kicked her under the table. She knew she'd screwed up the moment she opened her mouth.

Her mom gave her a puzzled look. "I haven't heard from Aunt Suzanne. I was going to call her this morning to talk about the trip. Did you talk to her?"

As if on cue, the cell phone in their mom's hand buzzed, insistently. Gen answered it. "Hey Sis, I was just going to call you." There was a pause while she listened. "Did you talk to Nadia already? OK. Hang on a sec, Suze." She turned to the twins. "Aunt Suzanne is fine with leaving Monday for New Hampshire." The twins nodded. Their mother stared at them. "How did you know that, Nadia?"

Nadia was a firm believer in the less-is-more method of deflecting parental attention. She put on her best I-don't-know-face and shrugged. Her mom's gaze remained on Nadia for just a second more, then, with a slight shake of her head, she turned her focus back to her phone.

"Why does she always let you off the hook and always think I'm hiding something?" Aidan whispered in Nadia's ear.

"Because you are." Her grin turned to a grimace as he gave her a playful punch in the arm.

A sudden movement from the window caught Nadia's eye and Aidan turned as well. Just outside, on a large rhododendron shrub, sat a big black bird.

Aidan said, "Wow, it looks like a raven, right there. Mom, look."

As their mother ended her call, she turned to look out the big picture window. "Yes, you're right. It's odd, though, we don't usually see them this close to the house." She turned back to the kids. "Did you guys know your dad had a raven when he was in high school? He found the baby bird on the lawn."

"Really? How come you never told us about that, Mom?" Heather slid two cookie sheets full of cookies into the oven.

Gen remained at the window, watching the bird. "I didn't know your father at the time, but I heard all about it. Your dad found it the day after your Grandma Catherine died."

"She must have been pretty young if your dad was only 15. How did she die?" Judessa asked.

"It's weird, Jude," Heather said. "She was 44. She died of a mysterious infection caused by a strain of bacteria no doctor had seen before. It is quite famous in medical circles – the CDC has saved samples of the bacteria and trials have been done with drugs to look for a cure. That's what my dad's been working on for almost 20 years. He's had a series of research grants to find a treatment that is effective against that particular strain of bacteria. Although he's worked with a couple of drugs that looked promising, he hasn't found the cure yet..."

Nadia chimed in, around a mouthful of cookie. "The weirdest part is that no one had ever seen the bacteria before. Or since, as far as anyone can tell. Anyway, that's what made Dad want to be a doctor, what made him specialize in medical research."

"And of course it is a big part of why I want to follow in his footsteps," said Heather.

Gen and the kids watched the raven lift off the shrub and fly away.

Heather shook off the offer of a cookie, sat down and made herself comfortable with a cup of black coffee. Nadia couldn't remember quite when Heather had stopped eating cookies, but it was looking like she would never eat one again. Nadia thought she was thin enough to have a cookie once in a while. Why did some girls get so weird about being thin?

Their mom left the window and came to join them at the table. "Your father loved that raven. He cared for it, fed it, nursed it. He kept his bedroom window open – he wouldn't keep it in a cage. The older it got, the longer it would take to come back from its daily flights, but for a long time it did. Then, just before he went away to medical school, it took off and never returned." She paused for a moment. "Lots of folks said it was his mother, Grandma Catherine, or at least sent by her somehow, to ease his broken heart."

Aidan snorted under his breath.

"I know you think that's not rational, Aidan, but stranger things have happened," his mother said.

Yeah, thought Nadia, like travelling through time.

"Hey, maybe this bird is the same raven!" Heather exclaimed.

Judessa nodded. "That would be cool! If it came back, I wonder if your dad would recognize it?"

Gen smiled. "I must remember to tell him. I don't think it could be the same bird, though – it's been over 20 years."

Nadia and Aidan shared a look. Was this the raven from the mirror? And if so, what was he doing outside looking in at them?

"OK, guys, I have to get going." Their mom stood up from the table. "Some errands to do." She grabbed her keys from the hook by the door, then turned back to the kids. "Just a head's up, you all need to plan on a half-hour family meeting tonight after dinner – ."

Heather broke in, "Mom, it's Saturday night – I have a date!"

Her mom continued, "OK, honey, we'll eat a bit early, like 5:30 or 6. It'll only take half an hour or so. Your dad has some news..."

"What, Mom? What's going on?" Nadia felt her stomach clench.

"We'll talk about it tonight. See you later, guys."

———————◆———————

Chapter 7

———◈———

Nadia wished their mom had not forewarned them about the family meeting. While they sometimes had meetings to announce good news, that was more the exception than the rule. Meetings usually meant a problem, something to be talked through. But, arriving at Corvid Books that afternoon, Nadia was determined to try to focus on the event. The book they were going to hear about was entitled, *The Power of Twins*, after all. Right up their alley.

The bookstore was humming. Nadia loved this place. Her dad told her that in this era of e-books, Corvid Books was a nexus for people who never bought into the electronic book age. He was one of them, Nadia knew. Reading for him had to involve an actual book with pages to turn. Aidan said Dad was just showing his age, that he was stuck in his ways, but Nadia really got it. She loved the feel of a real book, too.

When the twins arrived, their grandmother was already into the presentation. A popular figure in town, almost everyone who had lived in Cold Spring for any length of time knew, or knew of, Liz Shaw and Corvid Books. She was charismatic, Nadia thought. She should have been a movie star, she certainly was beautiful enough. Nadia was thrilled that sometimes people said she looked like her and had decided if she ever had to be old, she wanted to be old like Grandma Liz.

In her animated way, Grandma Liz was speaking to the intimate gathering of about thirty people, which included quite a few kids. "The phenomenon of twins has always fascinated us. There is a degree of mystery, myth, even a magical quality to it." She smiled as she surveyed her audience. "There are several sets of twins here today, including my own grandkids, Nadia and Aidan." She gestured toward them.

"I love their names – look at this." She grabbed a marker and wrote their names on a whiteboard behind her so all could read them.

"See? Their names are like mirror images of each other. Nadia is Aidan backward. And vice versa." The listeners loved this – there were smiles all around. Grandma Liz continued. "Pretty cool, huh? Their parents were clever!"

Grandma Liz continued. "Nadia and Aidan are not identical. They don't look alike, as you can see. But, they are very close and often even know what the other is thinking.

They were also born in June – their 13th birthdays were a couple of weeks ago – under the sign of Gemini. That's very powerful stuff. Gemini means twins."

Grandma Liz perched on a high stool, her long red skirt flowing over it, almost hiding it from view. With her long gray and black hair tied back with a red scarf and dangly earrings, she looked almost Spanish. Except for her pale Irish skin. She tucked a strand of hair that had escaped, back behind her ear.

Looking down at her feet, Grandma Liz spotted two young girls, about eight years old, sharing a large beanbag on the floor. "But I see we do have a set of identical twins here today." She grinned at them. They did look exactly alike: both had blond curly hair and both had blue eyes and shy smiles. "Identical twins can be astoundingly alike, but, they can also be very different people from each other, with different personalities. That sure was the case with my sister and me. You see, I am an identical twin, myself. My sister passed away many years ago, but I still remember what it's like to be a twin."

Nadia knew even though Grandma Catherine and Grandma Liz were physically identical, their personalities were polar opposites. She loved how quirky, outgoing and fun Grandma Liz was, but she had heard her whole life how Grandma Catherine was reserved, quiet and sophisticated. Yet, in pictures of them when they were young, you couldn't tell them apart.

Grandma Liz went on. "There are quite a few other identical and fraternal twins in our family, besides me – we are absolutely riddled with twins!" She looked down at the identical girls on the beanbag. "I make it sound like a disease, don't I?" The girls giggled.

There were an extraordinary number of twins in their family tree. Even Aidan and Nadia's parents were identical twins. Having grown up with an aunt that looked just like Mom and an uncle that looked exactly like Dad, Nadia was used to it. Mom loved to tell people about the time Aidan had made the kids in his English class laugh. The teacher had asked him to use the word ubiquitous in a sentence. He had thought for a second and said, "I have ubiquitous parents because they seem to be everywhere at once."

Nadia had often wondered if both parents being twins might have, in some way, contributed to the unique and powerful connection she had with Aidan, that whole one-plus-one-equals-three thing.

"Being a twin is sometimes quite magical, Grandma Liz told her audience. "Did you know that for some twins, when they are not together, it's possible for one of them to sense, to *know* somehow the other is hurt or in danger? It's as if there is a psychic connection. This is true for cousins of mine, one of the sets of identical twins that litter our family tree." She grinned down at the young girls again. "These twin cousins have the gift of precognition. But, and here is the weird part, it only happens for them when they are together, close together. When they are touching, this ability, this precognition, is doubled, or even tripled, in intensity. When the two of them hold hands and focus, they often *know* things. Before they happen!"

Nadia and Aidan stared at each other and Nadia mouthed, "Wow!" Maybe this is what happened when they were close to each other in front of the mirror, or holding the Ravenstone. Did that strengthen whatever bond they had?

"Like what, Mrs. Shaw?" A young voice called out from the back of the group.

"Well, my cousins knew their mom was going to be in a car accident. They felt it was going to happen – at any moment! They desperately tried to reach her to warn her, but her cell just bumped straight to voicemail. Unfortunately, the accident did occur. Don't worry, there were no fatalities, but their mom broke her leg and suffered other minor injuries. But, the kids had known exactly when and where it was going to happen."

Nadia had a hard time focusing when her grandmother introduced the author, who began to read from the introduction of her book. She was thinking about the magical appearances of the old man and the raven and the strange power of the Ravenstone. Were these things happening in part because of their *twin-ness?* Did they actually have some kind of power that was stronger when they were close together or touching? If so, could they use that somehow?

Nadia couldn't wait to talk about this with Aidan. The moment they left the bookstore, she blurted out, "The more I think about it, whenever we were touching, or physically close, the old man in the mirror was clearer."

"Yeah, and when we backed away from the mirror, the image faded," Aidan said. "And the Ravenstone only works when we are both holding it."

She nodded. "And then our thumbs touch..."

"Yeah, right!"

Nadia looked pensive.

Aidan said, "I know what you're thinking. What are we going to do with it?"

"I know what I want to do with it. I want to try it again!"

Aidan stopped up short on the sidewalk and stared at her. "I thought you were terrified of it!"

Nadia stopped, too, turned to face him and chose her words carefully. "Well, you know when you are on a roller coaster and it's racing up and down and you're scared out of your mind? You're screaming your butt off?"

Aidan grinned and they started walking again. "But, once you're off the ride, you run right back around to get in line to do it again?"

"Exactly." Nadia didn't need to say more. He got it. "So, we could go forward in time and see what high school and college are like. Ooh, Aidan, we could see what lottery numbers come up next week and go win the lottery!"

Aidan kept walking but rolled his eyes.

Nadia said quickly, "Think of all the people we could help. We could give most of it to charity... not keep it *all.*" She looked at him hopefully.

"Hang on a minute. I don't think we've been led to the Ravenstone to go win the lottery. As fun as that sounds." Aidan grinned at her. "But I have thought of so many cool times we could travel to and things we could see. We could go back and see what Cold Spring was like during the Civil War. Or, we could watch Henry Hudson sail up the Hudson River for the first time.." His voice trailed off.

Nadia was in a world of her own, thoughts whirling around in her head. "You know what would be awesome.

How about we go back in time and meet Grandma Catherine?"

"Whoa," he replied. "That's a little close to home."

"Of course it is, isn't that kind of the point?" Nadia looked at him, eyebrows raised.

"It's too risky," Aidan said. "We can't alter even the smallest detail of our own history. You know how every time-travel story you've ever heard has the whole train of events changing dramatically because of one small change the hero makes?"

She nodded.

"Well, suppose something we do means Grandma Catherine doesn't die? Then maybe, because of that, Dad doesn't become a doctor, doesn't go to medical school, doesn't even meet Mom..."

Nadia's eyes grew wide. "Oh yeah ... then we wouldn't even exist." Scrunching up her face, she grabbed Aidan's arm. "On second thought, let's not do that."

Aidan said, "Anyway, we don't even know how to use the stupid thing. I don't know how we got back to the present. We almost didn't."

"Yeah, but we *did* get back, Aidan. We must be able to figure out what we did, and do it again. Because we are supposed to use it, don't you think?"

He chewed on his lower lip. "You could even go so far as to say there's something we are supposed to do. We didn't just stumble onto all this."

"Uh-huh," Nadia said, nodding. "The old man in the mirror called to us, he came to *us*. There must be a reason."

"Yep." Aidan kicked a stone on the road and it clattered off to the gutter. "The old man will come back and tell us what this is all about..."

She nodded. They were quiet for a few moments. It was a beautiful warm day in mid-June and the beauty of spring was all around them. From a cloudless sky, the late afternoon sun cast its soft gold across the lawns and flowering shrubs of this lovely residential street, but the twins didn't see any of it. Lost in thought, they walked quietly.

Then they both spoke at once.

"Well, in the meantime, shouldn't we try it again?"

"Until he does, how about a practice run–"

They laughed. This happened often: same thought, same moment.

Chapter 8

———❦———

Back at the house, Nadia called out, making sure their mom and dad were not home, then followed Aidan upstairs. He stopped to listen outside Heather's bedroom and mimed that their sister was on the phone. That's Heather taken care of, thought Nadia. How can she talk to the same friends every five minutes? For hours and hours? She grinned as she hurried up the attic stairs.

"Ok, we have to figure out how it works," Aidan said.

Nadia dropped down to the floor and reached under the base of the mirror. It only took her a few seconds to find the little button that Aidan had described. She pushed it and heard the soft click as the hidden drawer popped open an inch. She opened the drawer completely and pulled out the mystical black stone. So, she hadn't imagined the whole thing; the stone was real and there it was... in her hands.

The two of them stared at it in silence for a moment, then Aidan continued, "We have to know what we are doing and we have to be able to do it every time –"

"And fast. I know..."

"No, not fast," Aidan cut her off. He held her by the shoulders for a moment and looked in her eyes. "If we hurry we'll only make mistakes."

"Ok... ok, I get it. Not fast." Nadia had to resist her impulsive nature. He was right even if he was a stick in the mud. "Where was I? Oh yeah, what were we thinking when it happened? Or what were we *feeling* – maybe that's it?"

"I think...," Aidan searched for the words. "I think it's like biofeedback. It should get easier each time. It definitely happened when our thumbs touched the first time even though we didn't do it deliberately. We must have been thinking or feeling or wishing the same thing.

"Exactly!" Nadia snapped her fingers and smiled, "That's why it didn't work right away when we tried to get back."

"Scared and rushing, we were each thinking something different and getting frantic. We weren't focused." Aidan stared at the stone as he searched his mind.

"Yes. I think that's it. When we got back to the right time last night, we were both saying how much we wanted to go home to the right time..."

Suddenly Nadia felt, or heard the words, *"One and one is three."* She glanced at the mirror, but it was still. They were on their own. But, she was sure she'd heard an old man's voice in her head. Nadia said, "I think the twins thing plays in, you know? The one and one is three piece about twins."

Aidan stared at her for a moment, then nodded. "But what if we are wrong and we get stuck? Can't get back?"

"Then we will be right here in front of the mirror and we will ask the old man to help us."

Aidan thought for a moment. "You're right. If we go forward say, one year, to this exact time and day, here in front of the mirror, then if there are problems we will ask the old man, or shaman, or wizard, or whatever he is."

Nadia grinned. "You're on. Let's do it."

They agreed to have a quick look around, make sure no one saw them, then come straight back, just to test that their theory of how to use the black stone was correct.

Nadia's heart was racing, partly with excitement, and partly with fear. She held the stone out to Aidan. He wrapped his hand around it and his thumb slid up along side hers. Aidan began chanting softly, "One year from today, same time, same place. I want to go to one year from today." His eyes were closed and she closed hers and tried to picture one year from today, 2017, June 17, same time, 4:30 PM. Exactly one year from today...

She felt the bolt of electricity, but it was much stronger than the first time. It shook her, took her breath away, and she found herself quaking with the power of it. She heard a cry from Aidan and her eyes flew open. He was shouting, "Don't let go!"

A huge golden arc swept up over and around them and everything within its reach glowed golden with its light. The mirror beside them disappeared and the walls and trunks and old floorboards of the attic fell away and vanished into the arc's light. The golden glow shimmered all around them and Nadia felt suspended in space as if she were lifted up off the ground. The roaring in her ears seemed to come from the light itself.

Then, as suddenly as it all started, the noise and brilliant light were gone but it was a moment before the feeling of the ground moving ceased.

"I think you can let go now." Her brother's voice brought her back to earth. She drew a deep breath and let her eyes take in the scene as her surroundings gradually came into focus. She glanced down and realized she was still clutching the Ravenstone so tightly her knuckles were white.

She caught her breath, but she suddenly gasped again. All around her the attic was different. It was empty. Empty!

"What?" Aidan cried, staring around wildly, then clapped his hand over his mouth. They must be quiet!

Well, not completely empty. The mirror, the trunks, the old rugs and bookcases, all the piles of boxes, were gone. The attic floor stretched out before them in a vast expanse. In all their lives they had never seen it without generations of family stuff piled everywhere. But, now there were studs and beams, the beginnings of walls dividing up the space. Two-by-fours and sheets of wallboard were stacked to the side and tools were piled in a heap, waiting for their owners to pick up where they left off.

"Wow! They are framing it out!" Speaking softly, but his voice full of excitement, Aidan continued, "Mom and Dad have been threatening to do something up here for years... to make another bedroom or something."

He pulled out his iPhone. "Yes, we did it, Nadia! It's June 17, 2017! Awesome!"

But then his grin faded. "We better go straight back, Nadia. The mirror isn't here. If we have a problem, we can't ask the shaman. Hey, what's up?"

"Something's not right," Nadia said slowly. She had not even heard the comment about the mirror. Something was up; her intuition was sizzling. As she headed towards the attic stairs, she said, "I need to just take a quick look."

"Careful!" Aidan followed her down to the door to the hallway and they both stood for a moment, listening. When they heard nothing, Nadia quietly turned the knob and peered out. Silence. She whispered back to Aidan, over her shoulder, "The table with that big flower bowl in the hall is gone, too." She pushed the door open further and flinched when it creaked loudly. They waited a few seconds and not hearing anything in response to the loud creak of the door, they crept noiselessly into the hall and dared to tiptoe along to the first room, Aidan's bedroom.

He gasped. It was empty! No furniture, nothing! Just bare bookshelves and wooden flooring. Even the blue and beige curtains that their mom had put up over Aidan's protests and eye rolling were gone and the naked glass panes made the room look lifeless.

"We're leaving this house? We're moving? Oh, no..." Nadia's voice trailed off.

Aidan grabbed his sister's hand to pull her from the bare room. They hurried down the hall, peering into Heather's room, their parents' room, the bathroom. All empty. Cleaned out.

Downstairs was the same story, except that the kitchen and dining room were now one big room – the wall connecting them had been torn down. It all looked so different! Nadia felt the shock in every cell of her being. That they could be moving, that someone else might come in to *their* home and rip out walls, change their wonderful attic, well, it felt like a tragedy. It didn't bear thinking about.

She felt sure she was going to cry, and that was not going to help anyone. She swallowed hard, a couple of times, as she followed Aidan into the new kitchen area. He was staring down at a piece of paper he had picked up from the counter.

"What is it?" she asked.

"Our forwarding address. In Montgomery, NJ."

Before Nadia could react, she heard the thunk of a car door shutting in the driveway. "Oh, no! Someone's here!" She raced through the kitchen to the foyer heading for the stairs, Aidan hard on her heels. Glancing as she ran, she saw through the front window a man in work clothes and a very big black dog just reaching the front door.

They didn't turn back to look, but raced up the stairs as fast as they could. As they reached the second floor, they heard the door open and the sound of scratching nails and growling closing on them, fast. Nadia shot past the empty bedrooms and through the attic door. Stepping aside to let Aidan pass, she threw her weight against the door as she pushed it shut. They both jumped at the sound of the growling beast slamming into the door at full speed.

"Rocky, what's wrong with you?"

The man's voice, loud even from the front foyer, warned them that they had mere seconds to get to the Ravenstone or they would be caught. They raced up to the center of the attic, where Aidan scooped the Ravenstone off the bare floor and extended it to Nadia.

She grabbed the other end. She tried to focus. Go home. The correct time. Go home. Oh, what was it she was supposed to focus on?

Then she heard Aidan's voice, "One year ago today, same time, same place." But his eyes were shut and his lips were not moving. He hadn't spoken, but somehow she could hear him. "One year ago today." She heard the words again in her head. She took a deep breath, and repeated them softly to herself, as she heard heavy footsteps in the hall right outside the door to the stairs, amidst the cacophony of barking.

Just as the door opened and she heard the monstrous dog scrambling up the last few steps, the blazing arc of light rose up around them, along with the deafening sound of wind and the shuddering feeling of electricity in her veins. She welcomed it this time. It didn't frighten her! It was a weird relief!

As the empty attic seemed to drop away, suddenly the huge black Rottweiler was snapping and barking right at her feet. And, for a split second, she could see the amazed face of the builder they had narrowly escaped, as he stood in the middle of their beloved attic.

At least, it used to be their attic.

Chapter 9

When the golden light, the noise, and the electric sensations faded, the twins were back in the attic, near the old cheval mirror. Aidan's phone confirmed they were back in 2016, at the same moment they left.

"We did it," he said, still out of breath from the race up the stairs. "We were right – we both have to focus on it at the same moment."

"But the empty house! Oh, Aidan!"

"I know...," Aidan said quickly. They heard the mudroom screen door slam. "Let's talk later."

Sitting around the table, everyone was pretty quiet. Nadia was convinced the family meeting that was happening right after dinner was going to be bad news. She just knew it. Was it anything to do with the empty house they had just seen? Having that hanging over her head had pretty much ruined her appetite. She caught herself gnawing on her thumbnail and, exasperated with herself, grabbed her paper napkin and began to wind it around and around her fingers. Anything to use up the nervous energy.

She gazed around the table. No one seemed to be enjoying the tacos, although it was one of their favorite dinners. Distracted, even depressed, thought Nadia, that's what I get from Dad. And nervous, that's what Mom feels like. Her appetite now completely gone, she pushed her plate away, rubbing her stomach gently, where a knot of anxiety was forming. The big, brightly colored kitchen was her favorite room in the house and usually made her feel cheerful. But, not tonight.

When the plates were finally all in the dishwasher and leftovers put away, her dad sat back down at the table and they all followed suit. This is it, thought Nadia. Her heart started to pound.

Her father gazed around the table at his family, sighed and began. "You all know things have not been going well at the lab." Indeed, they did, he talked about little else lately. "Well, this past year has been one disappointing dead-end after another."

Nadia wondered why they had to have a family meeting to hear this. It wasn't like they hadn't heard it all before.

"This year's results have been so below expectation," her dad continued, "that the CDC has informed me they are not going to fund my project anymore. Without their funding, the company cannot afford the lab space or my time to keep working on it. They are willing to keep me on in my capacity as a senior scientist and team leader for other programs but the Project is over if I stay."

Aidan made eye contact with Nadia and she sensed his apprehension. He looked back at their dad and asked, "What do you mean, 'if you stay?' Where else would you go?"

"I've been offered a position at a biotech startup company in southern New Jersey." Their father paused. "They've committed space and resources for my project to persuade me to accept their offer."

Nadia felt punched in the stomach and a stunned silence greeted her father.

"We know this comes as a shock and we waited until there was no other choice. But we have to do this," their mom said. "Your father's funding didn't come through... So we need to make a change. It will take a bit of effort, but I can practice in New Jersey and it is a very good position for your dad. There are plenty of jobs for nurses and I can build a new homeopathic practice on the side." Her voice was firm and calm, but she spoke too quickly, filling the silence with explanations.

Then all the kids spoke at once.

"But, Dad–," said Aidan.

"Oh, no, Mom, You guys kidding?" This was even worse than Nadia could have imagined.

"Isn't there any other funding you can get?" Heather asked.

"New JERSEY? Seriously?" Nadia was near panic. The move, everything they had seen a year into the future, it was all happening.

Their father held up his hand. "We know this is hard, especially for you two," and he looked at the twins. "Heather, you're off to college in September anyway, so this will affect you less."

"But Dad, this is *home.*" Heather protested. Her normally pale face had blanched, even whiter.

"I know, I know. Now, wait – hold on, everyone." Everyone started to protest again. "You have to realize this is hard for us too, believe me. This house was my mother's and her mother's before that."

"You aren't going to *sell* it?" Nadia slammed her milk glass down so hard that half of it sloshed out onto the table.

Her mom and dad glanced at each other.

"It may come to that," Mom said, "but we are hoping we can rent it, so we could return in a few years... or someday."

"Someday?" Nadia shouted. "*Montgomery, New Jersey?*" A new school, leave everyone, leave home and... everything?" She burst into tears.

Her mother and father stared at her, then her mom spoke firmly, "Now, Nadia – "

"Well, I am not going. I'm *not*. You can't make me! You CAN'T!" Nadia wailed. Jumping up from the table, she stormed from the kitchen and raced up the stairs.

An hour later Nadia was curled up, on her side, on the bed, amidst a pile of rumpled sheets and quilt. Nicky had tucked himself next to her, his head on her arm. He was purring like a tractor and as she stroked his soft fur, she whispered, "Oh, Nicky, it's awful, just awful." Big tears squeezed out of her eyes to drop on the pillow.

She heard her bedroom door open and peeked up, hoping it was not her mom or dad. Oh, good, it was Aidan. She sat up with her arms full of warm cat, who let his head roll back but kept right on purring. Nadia wiped her eyes with the back of her hand. "I'm not going. I'm *not*."

"I know."

There was a silence.

"It stinks, doesn't it?" Aidan said.

"Big time. Oh, Aidan." Nadia's eyes filled up again and she brushed hard at the tears. She stood up, abruptly, plopping Nicky down on the bed. He let out a little mew of indignation. She paced back and forth on the rug. "What are we going to do?"

"Well, I don't know yet..."

It was very close to dark outside and the bedroom was gloomy with shadows. Aidan flicked on the lamp next to her bed and Nadia winced at the sudden brightness. He sank down on the edge of the bed and Nicky, ever the opportunist, grabbed the chance to jump into his lap with a soft "Mrrroww." Aidan absentmindedly rubbed the big cat's back.

"I need to think about this," he said. "And maybe we should talk to Grandma Liz. She must know about it and she might have some ideas." Aidan paused. "And I have an idea, too, but it probably won't work, so don't get too hopeful. What if we could stay with Grandma Liz and Grandpa Art, at least for a while... maybe until we're out of middle school?"

Nadia sniffed and reached for a tissue. She blew her nose, hard. "Sounds great, but do you really think Mom and Dad would let us stay that long, if at all?"

"I don't know. It would put off moving right now, but eventually, we'd have to go."

Nadia knew what it meant. It meant she and Aidan would have to start high school in a whole new town, away from everyone they knew. And, they'd have to leave this house, the only home either of them had ever known.

She watched Aidan set his jaw and she knew he was determined not to cry, that he wanted to be strong for both of them. Well, she thought, they would just have to find a solution. There must be one, there always is.

"I feel like I'm going to explode. Seeing it in the future was one thing, but now, hearing them say it... it makes it so real." Nadia flopped down next to him and they were silent.

Almost joined at the hip, the twins could be quiet with each other, with no need to "fill space," as their mom called it. For them, silence was never awkward. Having each other near was an enormous boon to their lives and they knew it. They were never lonely, never had been. They had been snuggled up in their mother's womb together and had seldom been far apart since. They were each other's best friend. There were moments when they could practically read each other's minds, although Aunty Gran and Mom said Nadia seemed to be able to read anyone's mind.

After a few moments, Aidan took a deep breath. "Well, let's focus on the here and now. You know what Mom always says about trying to stay in the present moment..."

Nadia grumbled, "Yeah, but the present moment *stinks*."

Aidan threw her a look and laughed.

"We'll figure it out, we always do. And, we have each other. Remember what Grandma Liz says – we are greater than the sum of the parts."

"You're right... So, what is one plus one, Aidan?"

"Three." he answered with a halfhearted smile.

It was some time before Nadia could fall asleep. Her mom had come in to talk to her, to try to calm her down, before bed. Nadia didn't really feel angry anymore and nothing was said about her defiant outburst at the table. Her mother didn't even mention the odd fact that Nadia had known about Montgomery, New Jersey.

She wasn't able to help Nadia feel any better, though. Nadia had grown up aware of her dad's lifelong dream and The Project. She didn't need it explained to her again. But, her mom told her, once again, he had to go where he could continue to pursue that goal. Nadia's peevish, "Well, maybe he should go alone and come home on weekends," earned her a harsh look from her mother.

Then, when she finally drifted off to sleep, the old man's face from the mirror returned repeatedly to haunt her. All night, she drifted through a surreal dreamscape: a jumble of strange indecipherable words, which melted into giant black birds, which in turn morphed into Nazgul winging over Mount Doom. The old man's wrinkled face appeared again, this time, transformed into a Mordor-like wasteland awash in menacing marshes. Overhead loomed dark swirling clouds. Then, one last time the shadowy hooded figure appeared. This time, as he raised his head, the face inside the hood was her father's and she began to cry. She whispered, "Daddy, I want to go home."

She awoke with a start, when it was still dark, tears still wet on her face.

———————✦———————

Chapter 10

———————◆———————

After that haunting nightmare, when Nadia woke in the morning, she felt oddly calm and at peace. Her first thoughts were: We aren't moving. It's not happening.

She blinked away the cobwebs and as her sleepy brain woke up, she wondered if she was high on wishful thinking, or deep in denial. She had seen the empty house with her own two eyes. But, this knowing-things-before-they-happen thing was not very reliable and, if the events of the last few days had taught her anything, the future is a moving target.

She sat up and stretched, then slid carefully out from under Nicky, who was sleeping sprawled out over her leg. Mustn't Disturb The Cat. From her vantage point in the hallway, it seemed the entire family was still asleep, even her parents, who were generally early risers. Aidan's door was closed and she heard no sounds from his room. Of course, he often woke early and lay in bed reading or surfing the web on his phone before he got up. That was how he learned all that stuff he knew. She tapped, very softly, at his door, but there was no reply.

The attic door called to her. Hmmm, she thought. Why not? Just a look... Tiptoeing up the attic stairs in her stocking feet, Nadia approached the old cheval mirror. She stood in front of it for a few moments, but all that looked back was her own reflection. There she stood, blinking at herself in the tarnished mirror: a young girl in a wrinkled lavender bathrobe, puffy eyes from last night's crying and her dark hair mashed into a serious case of "bed-head." No old wizard and no raven.

As Nadia gazed at herself, her mind drifted and she wondered, if she and Aidan had been identical twins would they look like Nadia or like Aidan? Would she have been Aidan's twin brother or would Aidan have been her twin sister? She couldn't imagine life without her brilliant brother, just the way he was, so she stuck her tongue out at herself and chuckled.

She dropped down to the base of the mirror and retrieved the Ravenstone. She turned it over and over, studying the carvings and the molded places for her fingers. Then, without consciously deciding to, she suddenly stuck it under her bathrobe and hurried back down to her room. She closed the door softly and popped the Ravenstone into her backpack. She thought it would be fun to have it with her today, where she could look at it... But, maybe she wouldn't tell Aidan about it.

After breakfast, when Grandpa Art drove up in the Prius to pick them up, Aidan and Nadia were already outside, waiting. The atmosphere in the kitchen, at breakfast, had been a little tense, to say the least. Their mom had been trying to put a bright face on things. Much good that did. Nadia felt better outside.

"Hey, Grandpa," Aidan said.

Their grandfather climbed the steps to the porch and grabbed a banana from the wicker basket on the table.

"Hey, Aidan, hey Nadia, All set?"

"Hi, Grandpa Art." Nadia took a banana as well. She figured that a bit later on this morning she might regret not eating breakfast. "Where's Aunty-Gran?"

"Picking up some kids in the other car – we'll meet her out there."

"OK," replied Aidan. "Uh, Grandpa, have you heard the news?"

Art looked knowingly at Aidan. "You're talking about your dad's job, then?"

Aidan nodded.

"Your dad is a good man. When it comes right down to it, he'll do the right thing."

"I know he's a good man," Aidan said with just a touch of exasperation. "It just feels like he's doing what's right for him, not what's right for anybody else."

"He's in a very tough situation. If he follows his heart, it will affect all of you. But, if he does what is best for the family, he goes against everything he has dreamed of his whole life. Goes against the very driving force of his life. It's a hard call."

They were silent for a few moments. Aidan nodded slowly. Nadia chewed and waited. She knew Aidan was leading up to the big question.

"Do you know who Yogi Berra is?" Grandpa was always quoting people Nadia had never heard of. She wasn't sure where he was going with this and how it could possibly figure in, but Grandpa was like that sometimes.

"Kind of," Aidan replied. "Didn't he used to play for the Yankees?"

"That's right!" His grandfather was clearly impressed. "He was a great baseball player, but he was also famous for saying smart things in funny ways." Grandpa Art turned to face the twins. "And if he were here right now do you know what he'd say?"

Aidan and Nadia shrugged.

"He'd say, 'It ain't over till it's over.'" Grandpa smiled and winked.

Nadia glanced over at Aidan. She wasn't sure if Grandpa knew something she didn't or if he was just trying to make them feel better. It wasn't really working. But Aidan looked a little brighter. Here it comes, she thought.

"I've been thinking, Grandpa. Do you think... I know Mom and Dad won't like it, but do you think..." Aidan took a breath and just said it. "Do you think Nadia and I could live with you and Grandma Liz?"

"Now, Aidan, I don't know about that – "

"Maybe just through next year? We'll have to start at a new high school, anyway, after that..." Aidan's voice trailed off.

Grandpa Art grinned. "Well, you know I'd love it, your grandmother too. But, I don't think your mom and dad would be too happy about it. And they would probably say 'no.'" He stroked his beard. "Tell you what. Let me think about it and talk to Grandma Liz and your folks, OK?"

"OK, thanks." Now Aidan definitely perked up. Maybe he felt better thinking Grandpa Art was on their side.

Aidan climbed into the passenger seat of the car while Nadia raced back into the house. She returned in a moment carrying her purple backpack and jumped into the backseat. "Why do you always get shotgun?"

Her brother shot back, "Why do you always forget something?"

Nadia reached over the seat and gave Aidan a poke as their grandfather pulled away from the curb.

"Thanks for coming to Ninham Mountain with me! This area is the center of one of the most magical places in North America." Grandma Liz sat on one of the picnic tables, her feet on the seat as she faced the small crowd of a dozen or so kids and two or three parents. "I'm going to tell you a little about it, here, before we head up the trail. Ninham Mountain is the highest point in Putnam County. The early settlers named it Ninham Mountain after Daniel Ninham, the last chief of the Wappinger tribe."

Nadia smiled at Aidan, who nodded. She remembered he knew a lot about the Wappinger tribe, having written a paper for American History this last semester.

Grandma Liz continued. "To the Wappinger people this mountain was sacred. They believed that near the top there was a portal to another world and at certain times of the year they could communicate with that other world – or even enter it."

"What other world?" Nadia called out.

Grandma Liz flashed a brief smile at Nadia. "Good question. No one knows for sure. Some say it's accessed via the stone chambers up here. How many of you know there are over 500 mysterious stone chambers in the northeast and most of them are right here in the area surrounding Ninham Mountain?"

A few kids put their hands up, including Nadia and Aidan, who had often heard about Ninham Mountain and the stone chambers from their grandmother.

Jeremy, one of Aidan's friends from school, called out, "What's a stone chamber, Mrs. Shaw?"

"Perfect question, Jeremy. Come on, I'll show you." She hopped up from the picnic table and brushed off her jeans, knowing they'd rather look at a stone chamber than hear about one. "You can leave your packs and other stuff, but you'll want your cameras. And bring a bottle of water, it's a bit of a hike!" She started up the forest path leading from the grassy meadow.

Nadia tossed her backpack over her shoulder and she and Aidan hurried to catch up.

"Why are you hauling that thing up the trail?" Aidan asked.

Nadia whispered, "Tell you later."

The kids hiked along the pine-needled path, through ancient hemlocks, maples, and pines. It was cooler under the trees and Nadia loved the smell and feel of the soft pine-needle bed under her feet. One of her girlfriends, Melinda, was just ahead of her, trying to use her phone as she hiked. Nadia nearly bumped into her a few times as her friend slowed on the trail.

"You won't have much of a signal up here, Mel."

"You're right." Melinda sighed and popped her phone into the pocket of her jeans. "Hmmm, we really are out in the wild, huh?"

For half an hour or so the kids followed Grandma Liz up the winding path and Nadia started to feel someone was adding stones to her backpack. It got heavier and heavier. Just when she felt she would simply have to stop and rest and have some water, they rounded a bend in the trail and popped out into a tiny meadow. There, all the kids were gathering around Grandma Liz, near the opening to what looked like a cave.

"That must be it!" Nadia hurried nearer the group. Aidan caught up and they drew close to hear what their grandmother was saying.

"Stone chambers are like caves, built into hillsides, usually with very large capstones, that form the ceiling, like this one." She pointed to the huge stone over the doorway of the cave-like opening. "They were built so long ago there is no written record of who built them or why."

"What's so special about them?" One of the kids was peering through the dark doorway.

"Let's go inside – the sun's hot out here." Liz led the way in.

One by one, the kids ducked under the capstone into the darkened space inside. The interior was a cool reprieve from the heat of the sun. They gazed around, taking in the hard, bare earth floor and the huge stones that made up the walls. The area was larger than it looked from the outside, about 10 feet wide and 15 feet long.

"It's so big in here," Aidan said from near the door. He and Nadia were the last to enter the chamber and they remained near the opening.

Grandma Liz responded. "Yes, some of them are pretty large. And that's one reason why it seems a bit much to accept what many people say: that these are root cellars built by the early settlers." She gestured around the expanse of the interior of the stone-walled cave. "Geez, that would be a lotta roots." The kids laughed.

She continued. "Still, that's the ongoing explanation by the naysayers. But, there are also many people who think they were built by ancient Celts who sailed to the New England coast hundreds of years before Columbus. That brings me to another reason I have a hard time believing they are root cellars: why were they built so the sun shines directly in the doorway on the summer solstice?"

"You mean the first day of summer, Mrs. Shaw?"

"That's right, Josh." Grandma Liz smiled at the freckled boy who had asked the question. "Ancient cultures considered it to be a holy day. Also, there is something else kind of eerie. Strange things happen to a compass near the entrance to some of these chambers. They seem to go a bit wild. Like there is something magnetic, something inexplicable, that happens."

Near the doorway, Nadia opened up her backpack to retrieve her camera and as she looked in, she drew a quick breath. She poked Aidan and beckoned to him. She moved out through the door, to stand just outside and pulled the backpack open so Aidan could peer in.

"Look."

There was the Ravenstone, but something was different about it. It was glowing in the dark recess of Nadia's backpack, shining a slightly reddish gold color, as if it were hot.

"What the...?" Aidan whispered.

"Shh..."

He stared at it and then at his sister, then quickly popped the flap over her bag, so no one would see. They silently moved back through the doorway to the edge of the group.

Their grandmother was in full flow. "Many people who've hiked these grounds at night have reported strange lights that flash out of the ground. And popping sounds like someone walking on twigs – even when no one is there." Her small audience seemed engrossed at the possibility of mystery, of something paranormal or unexplained to do with these caves. "Even the skies above Putnam County are famous for the number of confirmed UFO sightings."

A pretty blond girl near Grandma Liz piped up. "Can we stay till tonight and see if something weird happens, Mrs. Shaw?"

Grandma Liz laughed. "Your mom and dad would be pretty upset with me, Kylie, if some aliens came to get you while you were up here!"

"But, it would be *awesome*." Kylie and her friends laughed.

Grandma Liz motioned for the kids to follow her. "OK. Come on, enough with aliens and spooky stuff, let's go eat." She headed for the woodland path toward the meadow, where Grandpa Art and the parent volunteers were laying out the picnic.

Aidan whispered to his sister, "Hang on, let them go on."

As the last of the kids disappeared down the path, Nadia flung open her backpack.

Aidan stared in at the glowing Ravenstone. "Wow. I can't believe you brought it!" He reached in and touched it quickly, as if checking a hot iron. Then he grasped it and pulled it out into the light.

"I know! It's warm! And look at it glowing!" Nadia was excited. "I wonder what that means..."

Aidan began to respond but suddenly whipped around to look back at the stone chamber. Nadia saw a flicker out of the corner of her eye and she gasped. There in the doorway of the chamber, floated an image, shimmering in waves, as if in water. Even as she moved toward it, with Aidan beside her, the thought struck her that it looked a little like the giant wavy portal in *Stargate.*

The watery image stilled, slowly, and the old wizard from the cheval mirror came into focus. While the twins stood watching, mesmerized, a montage of images played like a movie across the watery doorway.

First, the old man's image faded and in its place, the twins could see two kids, about their own age, dressed in old-fashioned clothing. The young girl wore a long pinafore dress laced across the front, shiny black shoes and a ribboned straw hat covering her blonde ringlets. The boy wore a rather stiff-looking gray jacket, knickerbockers with knee socks and boot-like shoes. In the image, they were standing outside the door of what appeared to be the very chamber where the kids were now standing.

Why are we seeing this? Nadia wondered. What did this have to do with us? Then she saw they were holding a black object and Aidan grabbed her wrist at the same moment. He must have seen it too! It was the Ravenstone!

Next, the entire image dissolved and after a moment, in its place appeared a woman, wearing a billowy cotton nightgown with lace edges. She was sitting on a carved four-poster bed, sheets pulled back as if she had been in bed. She was gazing down at what she held in her hands. She, too, was holding the Ravenstone! As Aidan and Nadia watched, she slowly pulled herself up from the bed, holding onto the headboard for a moment, as if for balance. She looked ill, very pale, and weak.

As the woman turned, Nadia could see her face. She looked liked pictures she had seen of Grandma Liz when she was younger. Could they be looking at an image of their grandmother from years ago?

As if reading her thoughts, Aidan whispered, "That's Grandma Liz!"

In the watery image, the woman stumbled slowly over to the cheval mirror – their cheval mirror! Then she slowly knelt down and reached under it, just as they had. The drawer slowly slid open and Nadia could make out the white satin pillow, inside. The woman gently placed the Ravenstone down on the pillow.

Nadia's hand flew up to her mouth.

Before they could react further, the image of the woman dissolved. It shimmered and settled and they could begin to make out a bearded man, in leather breeches over which he wore a boot-length brown cape clasped at the shoulder with an intricate brooch. The hood of the cape was drawn up over his head and Nadia tried to see his face – who was this? Why were they seeing him?

The man in the image slowly knelt down under a birch tree, to pick leaves of a low-growing plant. He got to his feet, holding a handful of the leaves, which looked like ferns in shape, but they were black. He carefully tucked the leaves into a tan-colored pouch made of what looked like deerskin, hanging from his rope belt. Again, he knelt down for more leaves.

"Aidan, Nadia, where are you guys?" It was Grandma Liz, her voice carrying through the trees. She was not yet in view, but coming closer.

Suddenly another voice, a deep voice, spoke in Nadia's ear.

"Come to Mystery Hill."

She jumped and swung around, thinking someone must have crept up behind her. Aidan had jumped, too, so clearly he had heard it. But, there was no one there, just Grandma Liz, now in view, approaching on the path.

"Come to Mystery Hill." The voice said, again, but more softly, as if from a distance.

Aidan suddenly whispered, "The Ravenstone! Nadia, quick, hide it!" Realizing the black stone was visible, quick as a flash, she stuffed it down in her backpack.

But, not fast enough. Grandma Liz had stopped dead, there on the path and was staring at them. Her eyes fixed on the backpack, her face was white. Her mouth fell open.

There was a silence, then Aidan called, "Hey, Aunty-Gran, we were just coming."

Grandma Liz did not respond. She stood, still as stone, both hands covering her mouth. She was staring at the backpack in Nadia's hands.

Nadia was suddenly flooded with sensations, like vibrations and words popped unbidden, into her mind. "There it is! Where did... All this time? How on earth?!" She realized these were coming from her grandmother and even weirder, she found she could identify the emotions behind these phrases as well. They came to her one after another like hammer blows: shock, fear, desire, loss, grief, guilt...

Wait, *guilt?* Why would her grandmother feel guilt? Before Nadia could figure out what to think or do next, her brother spoke.

"I'm hungry, Aunty-Gran. Let's go." Just as if nothing had happened, Aidan walked toward his grandmother and took her arm. Grandma Liz seemed to recover herself, somewhat, at his normal tone. She reached up to brush her thick hair back from her face and dropped her sunglasses from the top of her head into place over her eyes. The two set off down the path. Nadia could hear Aidan chatting about the stone chamber, how fascinating it was.

Nadia had always encountered some sort of wall when she tried to "read" Grandma Liz. But, today, it was different. She was still stunned by the rush of thoughts and emotions that had poured into her. Over her? At her? She couldn't tell. She had been able to read people before, but not like this. Nothing like this.

Chapter 11

"Aunty-Gran said there was power in the stone chamber. Boy, if she only knew..." Aidan shook his head, as he plopped down at his desk.

"Yes, it was so awesome," Nadia replied. "All those images, floating in the doorway. And the Ravenstone, it was glowing."

It was later that Sunday evening and Nadia was perched on the edge of Aidan's bed, while he booted up his computer. He had some Googling to do, he said. Their parents were safely ensconced in the den watching Masterpiece Theater, Heather was out, and the kids had grabbed the opportunity to put their heads together. They hadn't had a moment to talk privately until now, what with the picnic and just too many people around.

"I wonder... did the Ravenstone empower the stone chamber...?" Aidan asked.

"'Or did the stone chamber empower the Ravenstone?" Nadia shrugged. "And who were those kids in those funny clothes? And why was he showing them to us? And what were those funny black fern-like leaves the man was picking? What does that mean? And what's Mystery Hill? Did you hear that, too?"

Aidan nodded.

"I knew you must have heard it," she said. "And man, oh, man, Aidan, I got a boatload of emotions off of Aunty-Gran when she saw the Ravenstone. I've been dying to tell you all evening!"

Nadia got up and paced around the room. "I've been trying my whole life to read Grandma Liz and have been banging my head on a wall. Now, finally I break through and it was like walking into an avalanche!" Nadia stopped and turned to face him. "There was incredible sadness. And fear. Isn't that weird? Fear. And guilt... I mean seriously, guilt?"

Aidan stopped what he was doing on the computer and turned to look at her. "Guilt?"

She nodded.

Aidan said, "Wait, what? When you saw her face when she saw the Ravenstone, you got fear and sadness and *guilt*?"

She nodded again, then resumed her pacing.

Aidan said, "That's strange. What does she have to feel guilty about?"

"I know, right?" said Nadia, "Then just like that, she was back to normal. She acted like she didn't have a care in the world, all afternoon. She was eating and drinking and joking around like nothing had happened."

Aidan nodded. "Well, she definitely saw the stone. And yeah, it was weird her acting all normal and stuff."

"Yeah. And how did *you* act so normal when she got all shocked and pale?"

Aidan gave a little shrug and turned back to the computer.

Nadia plowed on. "I mean, you were so cool. I was freaking out and you just took her arm and wandered down the path with her, chatting away about the chamber. Blew me away. I couldn't get myself together that fast."

She plopped down on the bed and patted Nicky, who had tucked his head under her hand to have his ears rubbed. "Just so bizarre to have finally broken through that wall of Aunty-Gran's." She paused, her eyes far away. "I was wondering if it has something to do with the Ravenstone."

Aidan turned to her suddenly, his eyes opened wide. "Thinking the same thing! Maybe that we are using it, or holding it or something?"

"Or maybe that we traveled through time with it? Why would I suddenly be able to read Aunty-Gran now?"

Aidan shrugged and shook his head. "Why is all this happening to us? We said the shaman would have to come back and tell us more and he did! Sort of... but what does it all mean?"

Nadia shook her head. She pulled Nicky up into her arms and buried her face in his fur.

Aidan said, "Well, let's think about it. We know Grandma Liz knows about the Ravenstone. We did see her in the images in the doorway. That was her. So, she has seen it. She has held the Ravenstone before!"

Nadia held up a hand. "Wait a minute. Hold on! What if that was Grandma *Catherine* we saw?"

Aidan stared at her.

Nadia continued, "She was sick. The woman in the image was sick, wasn't she? And Grandma Catherine was Grandma Liz' identical twin. It could have been *her*!"

"Of course! Why didn't I think of that?" Aidan said. "Hey, why do you always think I am the smart one? Yes, I think you're right. Makes perfect sense."

Nadia could almost see Aidan's brain working, feverishly trying to add things up.

"Geez, that could mean..." He paused and took a breath. "OK, how about this? Grandma Catherine hid the stone. Clearly, Grandma Liz saw it in your hand today. What if they found it, held it... and did what we did?"

Nadia sat up suddenly and drew in a sharp breath. "You mean... Could she and Grandma Liz have *time-traveled*?"

"That's exactly what I mean." Aidan turned back to his computer. Having logged in, he opened an internet browser.

Nadia plopped Nicky down on the bed and went back to pacing back and forth. "There are so many pieces to this – I can't put it all together. Grandma Liz and Grandma Catherine – time traveled? Wow, it sort of ties my brain in a knot."

There was silence for a moment, except for the sound of Aidan clicking away on the keyboard. Then Nadia went on, "Then there are the two kids we saw, in those old-fashioned clothes. They had the Ravenstone, too. What does that tell us? They were in front of the same stone chamber."

She rubbed her stomach. "Yuk, too many barbecued spare ribs, I think. That was not even counting the potato salad, coleslaw and carrot cake I ate."

Aidan didn't turn from his computer screen. "Well, the Ravenstone was warm and glowing near the stone chamber, but not near the mirror... "

Nadia flopped back down on the bed. "And?"

"So, you were right," he replied, "it seems the stone gets the power from the chamber... or on Ninham Mountain, or something."

She nodded, then sat quietly for a minute, thinking. "And what's Mystery Hill?"

"That's exactly what I'm wondering. I'm looking it up right now," her brother said. "Got it. I was confused for a bit. It used to be called "'Mystery Hill.' They've renamed it – doesn't say why – and now it is called American Stonehenge. You know what Stonehenge is?"

She rolled her eyes. "Everyone knows what Stonehenge is. Those giant stones in a ring, in England – maybe Merlin built it, or something."

"Yeah. Created so long ago it may have even been thousands of years before Merlin. But, Mystery Hill, I mean American Stonehenge, this is here, in the US. It's in New Hampshire. And, it doesn't look anything like Stonehenge. At least from these pictures. Look."

Nadia jumped off the bed to look over his shoulder.

Aidan continued, "No one knows for sure who built it. It says, 'A maze of man-made chambers, walls, and ceremonial meeting places...' and it's 4000 years old, or more. Likely 'the oldest man-made construction in the United States.' Cool." He read for a moment or two. "It's supposed to be an ancient calendar, to determine solar and lunar events. But, it looks more like a whole maze of stone chambers, to me." He looked up at his sister. "And I'm not sure what it has to do with us." He clicked on a map link and quickly typed. "But, hey, it's near Nana's house in New Hampshire. It's only about half an hour from there."

Nadia said slowly, "We are supposed to 'Come to Mystery Hill.'"

"Well," Aidan replied as slowly, "we'll just have to do that."

Chapter 12

———◆———

New Hampshire

The twins always looked forward to their annual July or August vacation to see their other grandparents, Nana Jean, and Grandpa Morgan, who they all just called Pops. This year, because their parents were going to New Jersey to look for a house, the kids went early.

Too early for blueberry picking, thought Nadia. That was one of Aidan's favorite things about their summer visit to New Hampshire. But, now it was harvest time for asparagus and how she loved asparagus!

There were plenty of other great things to do, as well. The twins thought of it as summer camp – they affectionately called it "Hamp-Camp." Nadia chuckled, remembering that her dad called their New Hampshire time, "Factory Reconditioning," since Nana was strict about hours, manners and chores. The twins had long since given up even thinking about being lazy or disobeying, as Nana simply would not have it. But, Pops was a pushover.

And, as it turned out, finding a way to get to Mystery Hill wasn't difficult at all. The next afternoon, after the long drive to Nana's in New Hampshire, they simply asked her if they could go see it. She said she thought it was a great idea and went one step further. She told them there was a Solstice Eve Festival event there in a few days, on the evening of the 20th of June. She said it would be fun for them all to go.

Later, when the household had settled for the night, Nadia heard the lightest tap on the guest room door. Aidan had tiptoed up from the finished basement room where he and his cousins, Matt, who was 11 and Ryan, 12, were sleeping.

"Knew you'd come." She was in pajamas, but wide awake and sitting on the bed.

"Glad you're still up. How cool was that – what Nana said about us all going to Mystery Hill?"

"Yeah. Well, that was easy."

"I know. But, it's weird – it seems like everything is leading us, somehow, guiding us." He spoke slowly as if working it out as he went. "Ok, if that's the case, to what? Are we supposed to be doing something? I've been thinking – "

Nadia interrupted him with a groan. "Yeah, that five hours in the car."

Aidan grinned. "But lots of time to think things through."

She nodded. "And, yeah. There's a message in all this. There's something we're supposed to figure out. Something we're supposed to do."

"I know," her brother said. "Let's go through it again. Let's go back to the image of the man in the brown robe, who was picking some leaves or herbs or something. If we were meant to see that, there must be a reason. So, it occurred to me... Now, don't laugh, maybe I'm nuts, but is it just possible there might be a cure? A now-extinct plant we could go back in time to find? I'm not saying this very well – "

Nadia cut him off, jumping up from the bed. "Oh, that's it. That's *it!* When I saw that image, in front of the stone chamber, my brain said, "If the sick woman had been given those leaves she might have been cured. Yes. That really could be it."

"And maybe that herb, or whatever it is, could've cured Grandma Catherine."

Deep in thought, Nadia wandered to the window overlooking the front yard, where light from the nearly full moon streamed through the trees. She hardly saw it; her mind was busy putting a jigsaw puzzle together. "Then, it might be what Dad is looking for."

She paused and turned to face her brother. "Does this mean... that maybe..." She took a breath and just went for it. "That we could time-travel to a time and place where this herb is? Bring it to Dad somehow? Geez, Aidan, are we crazy to think this stuff?"

Aidan shook his head, slowly. "I know we aren't crazy. It all makes sense. We didn't go looking for this – the old man came to us. But if you're right, you know what this means, don't you?"

Nadia replied slowly, "It means... we wouldn't have to move if The Project was back on track for Dad!"

Aidan chewed on his lip. "We wouldn't have to move. Oh, man." He paused, his face screwed up in concentration. "If it's not too late, that is." He lay back on her bed, one arm thrown over his eyes. "I need to think about all this some more. But, if we're right about why we're seeing these images and why the old man showed us where to find the Ravenstone, then we will have to use it again."

Nadia took a deep breath. "Uh-huh. And go back in time. Find the leaves. And collect them to bring back."

Aidan sat up. "And not mess up time while doing it."

"And get them to Dad without his finding out about the dangerous thing we did."

Aidan nodded. "All this without knowing where we are going or what we will find when we get there."

Nadia blew out the breath she had been holding. "Or if we can get back."

"Yes, there is that," Aidan said slowly. "If we can get back."

Although there were chores to do every day, like collecting eggs, watering and currying Nana's four horses, and helping in her vegetable garden, there was plenty of time for fun. With Matt and Ryan, they went horseback riding and swimming or canoeing in the lake. There was a big game room over the garage, decked out with a pool table and even Pop's beloved 50-year-old pinball machine. He was a master and once again, Nadia watched Aidan try to beat him, a yearly challenge.

"Never gonna happen, Aidan," Pops said. "Bring it on, buddy." Then they'd play for hours, hollering at the top of their lungs. Nadia wandered off to read or bake apple-cinnamon muffins with Nana Jean. Nadia liked playing pinball for a while, but she liked books or doing something creative more than a competitive game.

She noticed that Aidan was distracted this trip and often lost in thought. There was a shadow over their whole visit, this time. The Move.

One afternoon, when the twins were stretched out in hammocks, reading, she asked him about it.

Aidan said, "How could there not be? How on earth do you do it? You seem to have left it all behind you in Cold Spring."

She thought about it for a moment, then figured she may as well go for it. "You'll think I've gone crazy," she said. "But, it's just not happening. We aren't moving."

"You can't stay in denial forever!" Aidan exclaimed.

Nadia looked surprised. "I'm not in denial. I just get the sense that we are not moving. I don't see it happening. Something will change, or something will save us."

"Yeah, right," muttered Aidan. "And what about the fact that the future says we're moving?"

She shrugged and shook her head. "I really don't know, Aidan. I know what we saw. Could that be one reality... one possibility? That doesn't come true, or something... because something is going to happen to change it? It might even be because of the Ravenstone." She paused, then picked up her book. "But, there is nothing we can do right now, so I am not going to think about it."

Aidan took a deep breath and sighed, "The Shaman told us to come to Mystery Hill for a reason. Maybe we'll find out tomorrow."

Chapter 13

———❀———

"I sure hope this is right. I hope this is where we're supposed to be," Nadia muttered, speaking softly so her cousins wouldn't overhear.

Aidan leaned in close to her ear. "We worked this all out. Don't second-guess the plan. He told us to come to Mystery Hill, this place used to be called Mystery Hill. What else could he have meant? There is too much coincidence everywhere for this to be a... a coincidence... well, you know what I mean." He chuckled and Nadia grinned. "You've got to have faith. Either way, we've got nothing to lose. If we're wrong, we just do a little sightseeing and go home."

They were following Matt, Ryan and Aunt Suzanne up a winding path through the trees, from the parking lot. There was a welcome center with gift shop and museum and just past that was a large meadow area where tents and booths were set up.

Nadia gazed around at all the cool stuff for sale: leather crafts and sheepskin rugs; Celtic and Indian jewelry; Native American drums; crockery and sculpture. Wafting through the air floated the aroma of food, such as hot turkey legs, fried avocado bites, and corn on the cob. There was even a place to sign up for a massage or a Reiki session in a tent set up just for alternative health sessions.

Hordes of people milled around, laughing, chatting and eating. Some of the people were dressed in medieval or new age costumes and it reminded Nadia of the Renaissance Festival Mom had taken them to last summer. A group of musicians played pan flutes and a woman dressed in a long purple robe sold crystals and amethyst.

"Awesome," said Matt, although it was almost unintelligible since he had already hit one of the food vendors and was mumbling around a mouthful from a gigantic turkey leg. "I'm going to try out some of those drums."

Aunt Suzanne handed him a Wet Wipe from her purse. "They won't thank you for your greasy mitts on the leather. OK, guys, let's meet back here in an hour." She turned to a stall where the proprietor presented her Native American turquoise jewelry. She muttered, "Oh, my..." as she glazed over and drifted off into the tent.

"Mom's down for the count." Ryan chuckled as he exchanged a mischievous glance with Matt. "Let the games begin," he said with a grin, as he and his brother took off toward the display of drums.

Nadia and Aidan were both too excited about their secret quest to think of food right now. They were here to see the rock formations and mazes of stone chambers. And what else? They had no idea what might happen, if anything. They just kept wondering why the old man called them here.

Leaving their cousins and aunt at the craft tents, they turned and followed the signs pointing the way to the main attraction at the top of the hill. They overtook a group of visitors, led by a smiling docent, who was deep into her memorized speech.

"The Solstice Eve festival is an annual event, colorful and great fun, as you can see. The nearby town gets involved and people come from all over. We get visitors from Massachusetts, Vermont, New York State – as far away as Ohio and Oregon!" The guide spoke a bit breathlessly, as she navigated the slightly rising path while talking over her shoulder to the group. She was a plump little woman with silver spirals of curls and a long flowery dress.

At a widening in the path, she stopped to catch her breath and turned to them. "Are you all having a good time? Food good?" As the visitors nodded, she grinned, her friendly face crinkling up with pleasure.

The guide continued, "Was America's Stonehenge built by a Native American Culture or pre-Colombian Celts? No one knows for sure." As she continued, launching into what was known (and not known) about America's Stonehenge, the twins realized they had read the same information online, so Aidan took advantage of the pause to slip around the group and continue up the torch-lit path. "We've only got an hour," he said over his shoulder to his sister, gesturing her to keep up.

"We may have more time than that, she's in jewelry mode," Nadia said. "Besides, it's not like she's going to leave without us."

They rounded a sharp bend in the path through the trees and came upon the main attraction of the site. Through the early evening shadows, they could see a maze of rocky chambers, some above ground, some below. It was built around a vast, flat section of exposed bedrock, like a Stone-Age amphitheater.

"Way cool," Aidan said.

It was much more impressive than the pictures Nadia had seen online, although it didn't look much like the images she'd seen of the original Stonehenge, in England.

"It's getting dark. Let's get the flashlights and head to that first chamber." Nadia dived into her backpack for one of the small tactical flashlights they had borrowed from their grandfather.

"OK. But be very careful with that thing,' Aidan said. "Don't look directly into it or shine it in anyone's face. It could blind them."

"You make it sound like a weapon, almost," Nadia replied.

"Not almost. It actually is a weapon. It is hundreds of times brighter than a camera flash – like 1200 lumens. Some tactical flashlights even have a strobe setting which can disorient an attacker."

Nadia rolled her eyes. He knew everything. And sometimes she had to hear about everything.

A floating movement distracted her and she looked up suddenly. There, right in the middle of the flat rock formation, she could see the hazy glow of a fire with smoke billowing up into the ever-darkening sky. She drew a sharp breath as her skin prickled and the hair stood up on her arms.

"What is it? Nadia?" Aidan looked to see what had caused her reaction.

"It's gone. But it was there, Aidan, a big fire – right there!" She pointed to the empty space in the middle of the circle of chambers, where a small group of people wandered among the shadows. "It looked kind of real but sort of unreal, like a hologram."

Aidan stood studying the spot where she was staring. "Wait, the stone," he said. "That'll help." He reached into his backpack, rummaged around, then looked at her and nodded. When she peered in, there, in his hand, was the mysterious stone. Yes! It was glowing. Keeping it away from prying eyes, he held it firmly, but out of sight.

Nadia looked up again toward the center of the stone platform. The fire image was back. Standing in the center and filling the flat rock formation was a shimmering circle of colossal granite stones, like pillars. In the center of that ring was a giant bonfire, arising from a great standing stone table, like a sacrificial altar. The blazing fire sparked and the smoke billowed up into the night sky. Shadows wavered across the massive stone pillars of the circle.

The word "Stonehenge" popped into Nadia's mind and she nodded to herself. Casting a quick glance over at Aidan, she saw the excitement in his eyes and a small but triumphant smile on his face. Nadia stared, mesmerized at this scene of fire and stone. It seemed to float and shimmer and she could see right through it to the people near them and the stone formations of Mystery Hill.

Then she remembered: the magic is more powerful when we're touching. She reached out and grabbed Aidan's hand. A rush of energy flowed through her, taking her breath away.

Instantly, the vision expanded, the circle of pillar-stones widened, as if she were moving closer to it. Or, was it moving closer to her? The sensation of movement made her feel dizzy and just for a moment it felt as if the earth shifted under her feet. She watched as the outer edges of the giant circle became fuzzy, distorted, and hazy.

She suddenly realized the tourists who had been milling around were no longer visible, no longer there! In fact, the rock formations of Mystery Hill, the chambers, the path and even the trees had disappeared. Everything beyond the towering circle of stones and the roaring fire had vanished behind a huge circular wall of clouds.

Aidan whispered, "My brain can't make sense of this. What's happened? Where are we? Did we somehow time-travel again?"

Nadia just shook her head. Absolutely no idea, she thought. Were they even still in New Hampshire? If that was Stonehenge and it certainly looked like it, could they be in England?

Her thoughts were interrupted as the vision before her continued to unfold. Figures slowly began to materialize just inside the stone circle. One after another, shadowy figures in gray robes appeared in a single, curved row facing the fire. Men in long robes, with large cavernous hoods, their backs to her, stood silently, as silent as the huge granite pillars above them. They appeared on the far side of the circle, perhaps twenty in all, soundless and faceless. The only sound was the crackling of the fire and the snapping of the sparks as they hit the cool night air.

Nadia was awed by this amazing scene but somehow felt safe. She could feel Aidan's hand in hers and he was right there beside her. She squeezed his hand and he glanced over at her, wonder on his face.

Just as she wondered what would happen next and if there was something she and Aidan should do, the hooded figure closest to them stepped away from the others, turned and began to walk toward them, staff in hand. She felt her heart begin to race in anticipation, or was it fear? He moved, ghostlike, through the pillars and with the glow of the fire lighting him from behind, Nadia could clearly make out the silhouette of a large black bird on his shoulder. The raven!

At that, the robed figure stopped, faced them and dropped his hood back down to his shoulders. Light from the bonfire flickered on his face. It was the old man they first saw in the mirror in the attic! The twins stood transfixed before the magnificent sight.

Nadia suddenly came to life and began to blurt out questions. "Who are you? Where are we? What are we supposed to do with the Ravenstone?" The old man held his hand up as if to stop her and gazed right at her. She waited and in the silence, she heard the answer, although later she could not adequately explain how she did so. The old man did not speak, but she knew what he was thinking, or what he wanted her to know.

"You are no longer in your time, yet you are not in mine."

Aidan said softly, "Do you mean we traveled through time?" Nadia realized Aidan heard the old man as well, but in his head, as she did.

The answer from the robed man appeared in Nadia's mind. It was unequivocal, even firm.

"We have little time. The power is fleeting. You must listen."

The kids nodded.

The old man raised his arms and as he did so, the raven lifted off his shoulder, pumped its powerful wings and took its place perched atop the tallest of giant sarsen stones. At the same instant, the ring of robed figures raised their arms in unison and the fire roared and sparked as if commanded by the men.

When the robed shaman next spoke in Nadia's head, it was as if he had truly called out into the night sky. The thoughts rang through her and filled her mind, her heart, her very being. Waves of emotion, energy, passion flooded through her.

"You were born to this path! This quest is your fate." Nadia and Aidan were breathless in the silence that followed this overwhelming pronouncement.

Then Nadia gathered herself to ask, "Is this about Grandma Catherine?"

The word "yes" did not appear in her mind, but affirmative energy washed over and through her. But, there came an additional thought, which altered the answer. Just two words, which surprised her.

"More than."

Before she could process this and ask another question, Aidan asked, "Then is this something to do with Dad?" And once again, although she heard no voice uttering the word, yes, she felt the rightness, the yes, in energy form. But immediately she received the thought:

"Greater than."

The twins looked at each other quickly.

Aidan spoke again. "Will Dad find the cure?"

"No."

Nadia was struck by the power of the negative energy. Then, the old man raised his arm and pointed his long forefinger directly at them.

"You will."

Nadia gasped. She knew it! The cure, the herb that would have helped the sick woman in the vision at the stone chamber – that is the cure that will help Dad. Her eyes filled with tears and she felt strong affirmative energy from the old wizard.

Just as she was wondering how on earth they were going to do it, to succeed with this incredible assignment, the old man pointed once again, this time to the Ravenstone glowing in Aidan's hand. Aidan sucked in his breath and clutched the stone even tighter.

As the twins looked down at the Ravenstone, it turned an even brighter reddish-golden color and began to pulsate. Aidan whispered, "We must use the stone."

As she watched it pulse, Nadia felt a prickling between her shoulder blades and a feeling she could only describe as a warning. The words came to her mind.

"Others seek it. Guard it well."

Aidan, beside her, nodded. Then both kids began to ask questions at the same time.

"How do we–?"

"When do we–?"

The wise old wizard held up a hand once more to hold back the flood of questions and, turning to the fire, he grasped hold of a long flaming stick, glowing red-hot at one end. With a flourish, he used the burning end to write in the grass and dirt before them, right at their feet:

459

Nadia heard the two words, *"Roman calendar,"* in her mind. This meant 459 A.D.

Then something snapped in Nadia. She felt her patience give way and her frustration take over. How can two kids find a plant, somewhere, a thousand years ago? She repressed a desire to stamp her foot, but honestly, this was huge! Her brain raced on. We have no idea what we're doing! Aloud she said, "How do we do it? Who will help us?"

As if in response, the old wizard sent her a clear thought. *"Seek Conall."*

Then a picture formed in Nadia's mind. She clearly saw the image of the man in the cape and the odd black fern in his hand. And the words *"warrior shaman"* floated into her mind.

The old man met each of their eyes, with meaning, clearly needing them to hear him: *Trust your gifts.*

Then he raised his staff and tapped the ground in front of him and the flames roared and crackled upwards toward the sky. The kids looked up and there in the smoke and the flames, they could see the image of the stone chamber on Ninham Mountain, shadowy and translucent about the old man's head. Nadia recognized "their" stone chamber and she gave her brother's hand a squeeze.

And the thoughts that appeared in her mind spoke again. *"The stone is more powerful in powerful places."*

The old man bowed his head and gathered his robe around himself as if the night chill had weakened his bones.

The raven lifted off from its perch atop the giant stone and floated down to land back on the wizard's shoulder. Its unblinking black eyes darted between Aidan and Nadia. The man reached up and stroked its glossy wing and Nadia sensed he gained strength from the bird.

The raven opened its huge beak and uttered a loud rasping "Graa." At that, as if a call to action, all the robed figures began to chant a series of long, deep notes, in unison, their arms once again raised high in the glow of the firelight.

The robed shaman shuddered and drew in a long deep breath as if mustering his reserves. The chanting ceased and all was quiet. Nadia knew the power was waning. There was not much time. The question filled her mind, Will you be there? Will you help us?

The old man lifted his face to them and the thought came clearly. *"Watch for the raven."*

With that, the image of the stones, the robed men, the raven and the old wizard began to shimmer, fade and shrink back as though being drawn toward the fire. Further and smaller, until all that remained were the last remnants of smoke and his parting message touching them through the night.

"Seek Conall."

Then, the old man was gone.

Chapter 14

———◆———

As the vision faded, the old man's voice echoed in Nadia's ears. Slowly she became aware of her surroundings. Shadows from the torches flickered across the flat rock formation before her, the fire that billowed flame and smoke into the air was gone, as were the stone pillars and robed men. She saw again the man in the yellow fleece jacket with his little girl, barely a step further than they were before the vision began.

Aidan, still beside her, said, "Did time just stand still for ten minutes? It looks like everyone was frozen in place." He glanced around at the other visitors, as though making sure no one was looking at them.

Nadia was dazed, as if in a waking dream. It had not, oddly enough, felt frightening. Why, she wondered, was she not scared? The answer floated up to her conscious mind from deep inside of her. She was familiar with the process; this is how it happens, she didn't need to force it. Somewhere between the sensing and the knowing, her "power" translated the feelings into words.

The essence of this feeling made her feel safe and the word that came to her was "goodness." Nadia was immediately aware there was nothing in the magical, out-of-time and place vision she had just experienced that was of darkness. Nothing that wished her harm. They were in no danger from the old man, from any of the monk-like men among the massive pillars of stone, and certainly not from the raven. They were of goodness.

The last bit of mist faded from her mind as Aidan grabbed her hand and pulled her over to a large bench-like ledge where they could sit and take stock.

He gazed back to the flat rock where moments before the great blaze had lit up the night sky and muttered, "Can you believe this?"

Nadia just shook her head a little, her hand up covering her mouth. "Did you hear what he said, Aidan? He said, 'This is your quest'... our fate."

"I know. It's incredible. I have to get all of this written down while it's fresh." Aidan pulled out his iPhone and began tapping out text. "Interstitial time... hope I'm spelling that right," he muttered under his breath.

"Huh? Interstitial time?" Nadia closed her eyes, lost in her own thoughts. Her heart was full of hope. Maybe they could help Dad. Maybe they wouldn't have to move. Maybe they'd even find something that would help many people.

"Yeah, I think that's what we could call it. I think we were in a sort of time between time." Aidan pressed send. "There. Sent it to you, too." He studied his sister for a minute. "Hey, you with me? Where is your head at?"

She opened her eyes to look at him. She said softly, "I keep getting that this is the answer."

Her brother nodded. "This is powerful stuff. We have to take it one step at a time. Right now I am so blown away my brain is rattling. Come on, let's walk."

The twins headed home the next morning to the Hudson Valley. During the long car ride, everyone passed the time differently. Halfway through the trip they stopped for a pig-out out at McDonalds, a rare event for the twins, whose nutrition-oriented holistic mom did not, to put it mildly, approve of junk food. Not as a regular event, anyway.

The kids occupied themselves on the road with audio books, games, and e-readers, while Aunt Suzanne listened to NPR as she drove.

Nadia was deep into *Watership Down,* which Nana had given her, telling her it was one of Aunt Suzanne's favorite books when she was a teenager. Nadia was drawn into it right from the start. A young rabbit named Fiver could sense some great evil was about to befall the warren where he lived with the other rabbits. But, no one would listen to him. Nadia could relate to Fiver's "knowing" and sensing. And, she thought wistfully, to being ignored.

When she checked in with Aidan, he told her he couldn't concentrate. He was trying to distract himself with an audio book, but he said he really wanted to be online, researching Native American tribes and their customs in the Hudson Valley 1000 years before Columbus. And he wanted to be collecting up all the items they would take on their trip.

Nadia stole a glance to ensure that Matt was focused on his game and Aunt Suzanne was still engrossed in her radio program. Then she looked over at Ryan, who was still asleep, with his face shoved uncomfortably against the window.

Nadia figured the road noise would cover their conversation, but she spoke softly. "Does everything you know about the Wappinger tribe help us now?"

"Maybe some, but most of that history only existed because the Europeans who colonized the area wrote it down. The Native Americans there had no written language. I have to try to figure out what life was like in the Hudson Valley in 459."

459. The very thought sent a thrill of nervous anxiety through Nadia. But also excitement. "I've got a pad and pen right here," she said. "Let's get organized." She dived into the back pocket of the seat in front of her and handed them to Aidan. He set about making a list. They quietly talked about what they should take with them to a time and place where none of the modern conveniences existed. Staying alive and safe was job one. Survival gear was essential, so they'd take flashlights, matches, water, power bars, a compass perhaps. Their cell phones would be useless. So would money.

How strange it was to think about all this, Nadia thought. Hmm, they would have to carry everything they brought. There would be no cars or bikes or even paved roads for that matter. They would have to travel light.

As Aidan wrote, Nadia's mind wandered back to the message of the old wizard. She had to trust him. She had to trust they would be all right, that he would not send them to their deaths... or worse. She tried not to think about all the things that could go wrong. She tried to focus, instead, on the goal and how important it was, to herself, to Aidan, to their father. She knew they had to do this, even if the risks were great.

Aidan asked, "Did you get a chance to jot down everything you heard? To make sure it matches what I heard?"

"Yeah, last night, before I went to sleep. Wait a minute. Wait, it's back there in my pack – I can't reach it now, but I remember it all. Boy oh boy, do I ever remember it. He said we will find Dad's cure!"

Aidan nodded. "Yeah, and that we have to guard the Ravenstone."

"He warned me that others will be looking for it. But bottom line, we go from the stone chamber on Ninham Mountain back to the year 459."

"And we heard the name 'Conall.' The warrior shaman. Did you get that?"

Aidan replied, "I heard Conall, but the words 'great healer.' One and the same, I guess. Cool that he spoke to us using different words, at the same time."

Nadia was silent for a moment. "I don't think he was actually speaking. I think it was more like telepathy. He put his thoughts in our heads and our minds translated them into words that made the most sense to us." She grinned. "It's not exactly a big secret that my brain works differently than yours. Something I don't get, though."

Aidan grinned. "Just one thing?"

"Well, if we are going back to 459 from the stone chamber to the same place... There weren't any Europeans in America then, right?"

Aidan nodded. "I know where you're going with this. How do we find Conall, right? That's a good old Irish name."

"Yes, exactly. It just doesn't make sense." Nadia chewed on her thumbnail.

"Well, we may have to take some stuff on trust," Aidan said.

"Yikes. Yeah, I guess so. But hang on, there's something else bugging me. When the old man first appeared to us in the mirror, why was his message in old Irish? He clearly can speak to us, or transmit his thoughts, in English."

Aidan nodded. "I think it's gotten easier for him to communicate, over time."

Nadia shrugged.

Aidan went on. "Or maybe it was a test."

"A test?"

"Yeah. Maybe he was never going to trust us with this mission if we were too stupid to work that out." He chuckled softly and she grinned.

"Maybe that's why he didn't help us with the second trip - when we went forward a year," said Nadia. "Maybe we were supposed to work out how to use it by ourselves."

Nadia's smile faded and she chewed on the inside of her cheek. Aidan studied his sister. "You scared?"

"Duh. Of course, I'm scared. Aren't you?"

"Hey, what are you guys talking about?" Ryan's voice cut in. He rubbed at his eyes. "Scared of what?"

"Nothing. You're too little to understand," Nadia said dismissively and turned her head to look out of the window.

"Come on," wheedled Ryan.

Aidan said calmly, "Well, if you must know, when we were at American Stonehenge, we crossed into interstitial time and met a wizard. He told us to travel through time on a mission to save the world."

"Ha ha, very funny, Aidan. You never tell me anything." Ryan slumped back in his seat and pulled out his Game-boy.

Nadia couldn't even look at her brother – she was afraid she would burst out laughing.

Chapter 15

——❀——

Cold Spring, NY

Grandpa Art turned the Prius onto the street where Nadia and Aidan lived.

"I'll water the vegetable garden and bring in the mail," he said. "How about you clean the cat pan and refill his food?"

Grandma Liz, in the passenger seat, was silent, gazing out of the window. He waited, but she did not reply.

"Hello? You with me here? Liz?"

Startled, she looked over at him. "What was that, hon?"

"What's up with you, Liz? You've been distracted for a couple of days, now."

Liz popped open her seat belt as Art pulled into the kids' driveway. "How about if I do the cat, OK? Can you get the mail?" Without waiting for a reply, she hopped out of the car and headed for the house.

Art shook his head and climbed out of the car.

Once inside, Grandma Liz darted straight up the stairs and headed for Aidan's room. First, she rummaged through the closet, then rooted around through the pile of shoes and boots on the floor. She was careful not to displace his things too much. Everything was organized and tidy in Aidan's closet. That's pretty unusual for a boy his age, she thought to herself. However, her grandson was unusual. Unique, actually.

Next, she scanned the various shelves above his computer. She peered behind the books, then moved across the room to rifle through the drawers in his dresser and desk. She went through his sock drawer and peered under the cushions on the window seat. Then she lifted up the mattress and reached under, sliding her arm in as far as it would go. She knelt and scanned under the bed. Dust and a whoopee cushion Grandpa Art had given Aidan at his recent birthday party was all she saw.

Standing up again, she stood with her hands on her hips, gazing around the room for a moment, then hurried to Nadia's room. She began the same thorough search there, although she did not take the same care in her granddaughter's room. Taking in the state of the room, she figured it would be impossible for anyone to know this room had been invaded at all. It was all a rather pleasant sort of energetic disarray, almost chaos. But, she probably knows where everything is, Liz thought, with a wry smile on her face.

She glanced through the jumble of tank tops, scarves, folders, books and CDs on Nadia's closet shelf and hunted around amongst the assortment of shoes and sandals. She hunted through her granddaughter's dresser drawers and even searched the American Girl doll collection in the antique trunk under the window. Nothing.

Outside, Art finished watering the carrots, peppers, lettuces and tomatoes in the vegetable garden, then carefully wound the 100-foot hose back up and carried the pile of mail inside. Dumping it on the kitchen counter, he muttered,

"Should just go straight in the recycling bin – what a pile of junk."

"Hey, hon, where are you?" he called out to his wife. Then he heard footsteps overhead. "Hey, Liz, I'm done. You all set?"

He heard her voice from the stairway, "Just coming."

Art reached down to stroke Nicky, who was yowling at him from the tile floor of the kitchen. Glancing over to the cat bowl, he noticed it stood empty. "You not been fed yet? Sorry, old boy, come on, let's get you some food." As he selected a can from the row of cat food cans in a cupboard, Liz crossed through the kitchen and headed for the mudroom.

"Ok, just have to see to the kitty-litter pan and we can head home," she said.

"What were you doing upstairs so long? Everything all right?"

"Sure, uh... I was just checking windows and stuff. Making sure everything was locked up tight."

Art gave her an odd look but kept his thoughts to himself. Changing the subject, he asked, "Have you thought any more about the twins living with us for a year, till they finish middle school?"

Grandma Liz sat up on her haunches, from where she was kneeling, litter-shovel in hand. She threw him a quick glance. "You know, the more I think about it, the more I believe it's a terrific idea if Michael and Gen would agree."

"I think so too. That's great, honey. Well, I will sit Michael down when they get back from New Jersey and see what they have to say about it."

For a few moments, there were just the sounds of Nicky wolfing down his food and Liz scraping away in the litter pan.

Grandpa Art said, "Yes, I will have a talk with him." He scratched his beard and continued quietly, more to himself than his wife. "I wonder if he knows what moving them will do to those kids."

———————⬥———————

Chapter 16

———————❁———————

Nadia felt as if they'd been away for a month. Heather was off somewhere with Judessa, doing whatever 17-year-old girls do and Dad wasn't home yet, so the twins were on the porch, waiting for Mom to get home from the clinic.

The kids had put their heads together, researched online and had worked out all the details they could think of. They'd filled their backpacks, ready for the big trip.

"I got the Power Bars and put a few in each pack," said Aidan.

His sister nodded absentmindedly. Clearly, her mind was elsewhere.

"What?" Aidan asked.

"Well, I forgot to tell you. I think someone looked through my room while we were gone."

Aidan's eyes opened wide. "Mine, too. My sock drawer all a-jumble, the pillows on the window seat were moved, stuff like that."

Nadia sometimes teased him for being so organized and tidy, just as he called her a slob. But, she knew he liked things the way he liked them. He liked logical places for things, having his things where they belonged. Helped him think, he said.

"As soon as I walked in, I knew," Nadia said. "Not sure how exactly. Things were just a bit out of place. Don't say it – how would I know? I know, my room is usually a bit of a mess." OK, a lot of a mess, she thought. "The clock on my nightstand was turned funny. And, an old sweatshirt I haven't worn for ages had fallen onto the closet floor. How could that have happened? Nicky can't get up there."

Besides these items that were out of place, it was more that she could feel it, *sense* it. Someone had searched her room. She cocked her head slightly to one side. "Aunty-Gran looking for the Ravenstone?"

"Uh-huh," replied Aidan. "I think so. Nobody else was in the house while we were gone and we both know she saw it that day at the stone chamber. And you saw how she reacted."

"So, what do we do about that?" asked Nadia.

Aidan seemed to concentrate, then gave a slight shrug. "I got nuttin," he muttered, which made Nadia grin.

Then they couldn't talk anymore, as their Mom arrived home, jumping out of her car to give them big hugs. It was as if they had been gone a year, instead of five days, thought Nadia. But, a hug from her mom felt so good. She wished, just a bit, that they'd never seen the old man in the mirror, that they had never found the stone. That they'd never time-traveled. If only things could just go back to how they were a week ago. Geez, she thought, shocked, all this has only been a week.

They sat on the porch with their mom, mango-flavored ice teas in hand. Nicky jumped up on Nadia's lap and began to purr ecstatically. Nadia caught her mother up with all the fun things they did in New Hampshire. A lot had happened, but the most important piece, of course, she could not share.

The happy atmosphere seemed a bit artificial, with everyone trying to ignore the elephant in the room. No one had brought up the dreaded Move. Their mom had said nothing about the New Jersey visit to see houses, even when Aidan hesitantly asked how it went. "Fine." was the short reply, accompanied by a big breezy smile and another query about kayaking. Their mother was skillfully chatting circles around the subject, keeping it just out of reach.

Nadia was glad when the talk was interrupted by a car horn and she turned to see her father's Leaf turning into the driveway. Her dad climbed out of the car, slowly straightening with an effort and waved at them.

"Hey, guys. Welcome home. We sure missed you."

Nadia sensed his gloom, it washed over her as he spoke. Oh no, she thought, something's wrong. Is Dad all right? She couldn't narrow it down to anything specific, just the heavy feeling of sadness and tiredness coming from her father. No one else seemed to notice.

Aidan and her mom jumped up to greet him. Then, Nadia gave her dad a hug and the feeling intensified as he put his arms around her and gave her a big squeeze.

"How's my little muffin?" he whispered in her ear.

"Oh, Daddy, I'm so sorry I was so awful before we left."

"It's OK, honey, I understand. It's all right. Just hug your old dad."

Gen put a cold beer in her husband's hand, smiled and kissed him on the cheek. Michael sat down in a big wicker chair, flopping his briefcase on the porch floor beside him. Nicky leaped up on his lap and Michael idly pet the big cat.

"So, good trip?" their dad asked.

Before Nadia and Aidan could begin to tell him, their mother cut them off.

"Honey, just tell them, please. I can't stand another minute of this."

There was a pause while the twins stared at their parents. Then their dad nodded.

"You're right, Gen." He dumped Nicky off onto the floor, stood up again and walked to the edge of the porch. He stood looking out over the lawn, now streaked with late afternoon shadows. Without turning, he said quietly, "We are not moving."

Nadia was flooded with relief. "Oh, Daddy," she said softly. She'd known all along that something would happen to stop the move!

The twins locked eyes, and when she felt Aidan's confusion, she knew she had to cover. She jumped up and ran to her dad. "That's awesome! What happened? Did the clinic reconsider and give you the funding?"

"No. I wish... No, I just decided it's time. It's time I let The Project go. I'm done with it. I've taken it as far as it can go."

Nadia felt the untruth behind the words, but also the love and kindness. Her eyes filled with tears. She knew the real reason for this decision. He was doing this for them. He was putting them ahead of his dream, the goal he had been working on for his entire life.

As a red Prius pulled into the driveway, her mom said, "It's Grandma Liz. She and Grandpa are coming over to have pizza with us and welcome you guys home." She waved and Grandma joined them all on the porch.

"Hi, Gen. Hi, Michael," Grandma Liz said. "Grandpa is picking up the pizzas, should be here in 15 or so." She turned to Aidan and Nadia. "And how are my favorite twins? I can't wait to hear all about your trip, you two, but let's hold it till he gets here – so you don't have to tell it twice." She grinned and gave them a hug.

"OK, I'll go get showered and changed," their mom said. Would you kids get the table ready? Heather should be home in a few minutes, too. We can talk about all this over dinner. It is wonderful news – I knew you would be thrilled." She disappeared into the house.

The twins and Grandma Liz left Michael on the porch with his paper and beer and headed for the kitchen to set the table. And Nadia knew there was a carrot cake in the fridge she had spied earlier. All that sugar! Mom must have really missed them. She smiled to herself.

"Glad to have a few minutes with you guys," Grandma Liz said. "We need to talk."

Nadia's grin vanished and she felt her stomach clench. She turned to face her grandmother, who was choosing a big red and white mug from the rack on the counter. She poured herself a cup of black coffee from the carafe.

Nadia had never been able to read her Grandma Liz until the day at the stone chamber and then it had come through like a tidal wave. Would it work again now? She briefly closed her eyes and focused on her grandmother. After a moment, she got a sense of anxiety... and fear. What was Aunty-Gran afraid of?

Nervous and perplexed, Nadia glanced across at her brother. He looked at her hard and gave a furtive shrug. Nadia understood: It is what it is. Trust me. Let me do this one. She felt a wave of love and gratitude for her brother. I mean, he was her big brother. Ha ha! Older by an entire two minutes and forty seconds.

As Grandma Liz settled herself at the kitchen table, motioning them to join her, Aidan asked, "Did you search through my room?"

Liz sloshed hot coffee over her hand. "Ow!" She hurried to the sink to run cold water over the burn.

Nadia could sense her grandmother's dismay and felt a bit awkward about it. Aunty-Gran always meant well and Nadia could tell that was the case this time, too. It was just that there was an undercurrent of something else running along with the goodwill. Again, she sensed fear, but also, oddly enough, guilt, from her grandmother.

"Did you?" Aidan asked again, a bit more forcefully.

"I don't care for your tone, young man." She paused. "I want to talk with you about the stone artifact you found."

Aidan tried to cover his initial look of shock. Nadia knew his plan was, "offense is the best defense," but it had backfired a bit. She sure hadn't thought her grandmother would go straight at it, like that. Oh, no, I hope we aren't going to have a showdown of some sort with Aunty-Gran. Nadia wished so much that she could tell her everything.

Grandma Liz turned from the sink, drying her hands on a towel. "It looked familiar when I saw it out on Ninham

Mountain. I knew I'd seen it before, but I couldn't quite remember where. Then it came to me. My grandmother, Nora, was an artist. I have some of her paintings and sketchbooks at home. That stone is pictured in one of her sketches."

Nadia felt the lie in the sentence, but she didn't know which part was untrue. Her sense was that her grandmother knew a lot more than she was telling about the stone, but was playing it very cool. So much for wishing she could tell her grandmother all about it. Something was really wrong, here.

"We need to show it to your mom and dad. Or, maybe you should give it to me and I will keep it safe, get it appraised. It is probably valuable, it is certainly an antique, even a family heirloom..." Grandma Liz trailed off, but she was watching them closely.

She wants to know what we know, thought Nadia. Her radar was humming.

Her grandmother seemed calm, on the outside, but Nadia could feel a swirling tempest of emotions. So, she took a chance. "Aunty-Gran, why are you upset about this? You seem scared, or guilty."

"Guilty? Don't be ridiculous." Grandma Liz' voice carried an edge and she stood up, sharply, her chair scraping against the tile as she shoved it back from the table. "And I'm not upset. But this could be a valuable artifact, it's not a toy."

"We didn't do anything wrong, Aunty-Gran," Nadia said. "Why are you mad at us?"

"Honey, I'm not angry with you. I am just afraid that you might accidently do something you can't undo – " Liz stopped suddenly, then went on, quickly, "I mean, if you lost it, or something."

It struck Nadia again: Grandma Liz' intentions were good but something did not ring true. She'd have to think about it later. Right now, they had to get out of this, somehow, with the Ravenstone still in their possession. And, somehow, without lying to their grandmother.

Aidan said quickly, "OK, you're right, Aunty-Gran. We probably should have taken it to Mom and Dad, but we just thought – "

"Hey guys, welcome back!" It was Grandpa Art. The twins and Grandma Liz turned to see him in the doorway, carrying boxes of pizza, a plastic bag, and a wrench. "Great news, huh, that you aren't moving?" he continued. "And I brought that new showerhead to replace the messed up one in the downstairs bath. I know you don't need to show the house now, but heck, I was going to fix it for perfect strangers but why shouldn't I fix it for my favorite grandchildren?" He laughed.

When no one laughed with him, Grandpa Art studied each of them in turn. "What's going on, Liz?"

Aidan grinned at his grandfather. "Oh, nothing, Grandpa, Nadia and I were just chatting to Aunty-Gran. Hey, Heather!"

Heather came bustling through the back door of the mudroom, carrying big shopping bags. "Hey, guys! Did you two have fun up at Hamp-Camp? You'll have to tell me all about it. I've been to the outlet stores and yowsa, I took a haul! Great stuff – have to show you, Nadia."

Good timing, Nadia thought.

In the welcoming bustle, Heather chatted on happily, oblivious to the tense atmosphere. "Mom will freak when she sees the credit card, but it's all for school, so should be OK. I'm starved, when's dinner?"

Aunty-Gran spoke softly near Nadia's ear. "We aren't done talking about this. I'll see you two tomorrow." Then she grinned merrily at her older granddaughter. "I want to see all your goodies, too, Heather!"

Well, Dad said they were not moving. That should have fixed everything, Nadia thought. They were off the hook and the looming threat of moving to New Jersey was gone. Just as she'd sensed. Something had happened to change the future, just as she told Aidan.

The twins had a chance to talk, for a few minutes, before they went to bed.

"You were right," Aidan said. And I've been thinking... there might be a simple explanation. I wonder if the truth is that we could travel four different times and see four different futures because the future isn't set in stone. Anything that happens in between can change the future."

Nadia shrugged. "Maybe so. But, we'll probably never really know."

Later, lying in bed trying to get to sleep, Nadia watched the clock creep toward midnight. Something was still bugging her. With them not moving, did that mean they didn't have to face the dangerous adventure through time? The old man had spoken only of finding the cure; the move to New Jersey never came up. It wasn't even part of the equation. Her dad was planning to abandon the project he had worked on for 20 years so Aidan and Nadia wouldn't have to make new friends. The thought of it made Nadia feel small and selfish. How could they stand by and let it happen when they'd been given a chance to change everything?

Besides, there was more at stake here. The old man was clear that this was about more than Grandma Catherine and more than Dad. It was much bigger than just two people and it was clearly bigger than whether they were moving to New Jersey or not. There was a greater purpose to this mission. It was their fate.

Also, Aunty-Gran might take the Ravenstone from them. What to do about that?

Wow, I really need to talk to Aidan, she thought.

As if on cue, there was a soft knock and Aidan popped his head around the door.

"Oh, good, you're still up. I can't sleep," he whispered, closing the door softly.

"Me neither. And I know why."

"Me too."

Aidan sat on the edge of the bed and the twins stared at each other. Since before birth, their lives were intimately interwoven. At times, when something big, something important affected them they were of one mind. This was one of those times and the look in each other's eyes confirmed it.

"Whether we move or not, whether the future we saw was real or not–" Nadia said.

"Doesn't change a thing." said Aidan.

"Nope."

"OK, let's plan this. I think we should go now. Tonight. Aunty-Gran might demand we give her the Ravenstone tomorrow."

Nadia agree. "Yikes. You're right." She thought for a moment. "OK, we have to go now. But let's wait 'til the middle of the night."

"Yeah. Perfect. We have the world's best flashlight and great lights on our bikes."

Chapter 17

———◆———

The big moment was imminent. Nadia and Aidan had crept out of the house at 2 a.m. and covered the distance to Ninham Mountain with surprising ease. When the streetlights ended, they found they could see well with the bike headlamps. There was hardly anyone on the road, but twice when they saw headlights in the distance, they ducked behind some trees beside the road until the car had passed. When they had ridden as far as they could on pavement, they hopped off their bikes and pushed them along the woodland trail toward the stone chamber.

Nadia was still thinking about Grandma Liz. "That was so weird. She acted as if she were calm, but she was scared and upset. I wish we knew for sure how much Aunty-Gran knows about the stone. Do you think it's possible she time-traveled with the Ravenstone?"

"I think it's more than just possible and I think something bad happened." Aidan sounded sure.

"Well, we can't ask her – she'd never let us keep it if she knows we've used it." Nadia was quiet for a moment and then said, "Grandma Liz didn't know where the stone was or she would have found it right off and she wouldn't have needed to search our rooms. So, that means…"

"It means the woman in the vision who we saw putting the stone in the mirror was Grandma Catherine."

"Exactly." Nadia thought for a moment. "And just maybe Grandma Catherine hid it from Aunty-Gran. Wow, I wonder why."

"Well, how about this? We know Grandma Catherine got sick and died from some strange bug. Maybe she got it in some other time… or place."

"Geez, that's a scary idea." Then she laughed. "Hey, way to reassure me, Aidan!"

Approaching the stone chamber, they found a place to hide the bikes in a clump of small pines.

"Hiding our bikes might not even be necessary. If everything goes right we'll arrive back here at this exact moment," mused Aidan.

Nadia slipped off her backpack, reached in and pulled out the Ravenstone. It was glowing and warm to the touch.

The twins had discussed this moment countless times, the moment they would launch themselves over fifteen centuries back through time. They could still hardly believe it was going to happen. They had tried to take into consideration every possible thing that could go wrong, but now that the moment was here, Nadia knew they couldn't possibly think of everything. At some point, they were just going to have to wing it.

"I don't want to put it off," she said. "Let's not talk about it anymore, let's just *do* it."

"I think we're as ready as we'll ever be." This response made sense, but Aidan did not sound nearly as confident and encouraging as Nadia had hoped. Her heart was in her throat, as if she were waiting in line at one of the giant rides at Disneyworld.

Holding the Ravenstone like a Geiger counter, Nadia walked the few steps through the doorway and into the chamber, then turned and, retracing her steps, stopped directly in the doorway itself. "This is it." She locked eyes with Aidan. "More powerful in powerful places, that's what he said... This is the spot, it glows the brightest right here."

"Well, we're going to need all the power we can get," Aidan said firmly.

"OK. Focus in on the year 459. 10 a.m. Morning of the same day, June 22. Same place, right here," Aidan pointed at the ground where they stood. They had decided to take as many variables as possible out of the mix. The less there was to think about, the less there was to screw up, Aidan had said. Fifteen hundred and fifty-seven years ago was enough to hold in their heads.

Nadia held the Ravenstone out to Aidan. "I am picturing 459, June 22, 10 in the morning." She put her heart and mind into it, concentrating on her desire to go to that time and that place.

Aidan took a deep breath and slid his hand into the grooves on the black stone. As his eyes closed, his thumb touched his sister's.

The bolt of electricity was even greater than the first two times they had used the stone. Nadia could barely breathe from the power of it. But, she stayed calm and focused on their goal. She knew they could do it.

The huge golden arc loomed around them and the doorway of the chamber fell away. The forest and meadow vanished and all she could see was golden light and all she could hear was a roaring sound, as if from a great wind. The golden glow of the arc shimmered all around them, then expanded into a winding path of light undulating into the vast darkness beyond. Then they were slowly drawn along this brilliant shining path.

When the noise and light faded, they could begin to make out their surroundings. Nadia waited for the eerie sensation of the earth moving to stop, then drew a deep breath and let her eyes take in the scene.

She looked out from where they stood, still in the doorway of the stone chamber. It was daylight, a cloudy day, as if rain was not far off. Immediately in front of the stone chamber, instead of the empty, grassy clearing they were used to, there was a carefully organized area that looked as if it was used for ceremonies. Hanging from the monolith just across from the door was a limp garland of wild flowers, faded and dry, as if a few days old. In the center of the clearing was a fire pit with the remains of a recent fire and to the side stood an alter-like stone table. Ringing the fire pit sat a dozen intricately carved wooden stumps that must be used as seats.

It had worked again! But, were they really back in time?

Aidan stood staring at their suddenly changed surroundings, then turned to Nadia and said with a smile. "Hey, Toto… I have a feeling we're not in Kansas anymore." He grabbed Nadia for a hug. "We gettin' good at this!"

"But is it 459?"

Aidan didn't reply. He had turned back to peer into the chamber. When Nadia turned to see what he was doing, she saw what had caught his eye. In the shadowy interior of the chamber, she could see the walls were stained a deep golden tan color and images in various colors appeared to be painted on that plain wash.

Aidan pulled the flashlight out of his backpack to flick the bright white light around the chamber.

There before them, filling the back wall were gray and black Tree of Life and Celtic knot images and on the walls to either side, Nadia could make out painted images of animals, in soft blue and peach colors: a coyote, a mother deer with a little spotted fawn, a black-masked raccoon, an elk, and a large raven.

"Wow," muttered Aidan.

"Come on, let's get going." Nadia pulled at his sleeve. Now that the time-travel was behind them, for the moment, she wanted to get on with it, to stay focused. Looking at cave paintings was all very well, but she was nervous and standing around when they had things to do wasn't helping. "Let's go find Conall."

Heading down the mountain was a no-brainer and they had decided to head toward the Hudson River, where there would be settlements of Indians, early Wappinger tribe, or Algonquin family.

"I sure hope they're friendly," he said. "If we really have traveled all the way back to 459, the Indians will never have seen anything like us!" He reached into his pack for the compass he had packed, only to notice that Nadia already had hers in her hand.

"I assume we're going west," she said, "and this path leads almost directly west."

"Yup. Sounds good to me, Sherlock." When his sister pointed her finger, Aidan gestured with a grand sweep of his arm indicating she should take the lead.

They set off along a woodland trail leading away from the clearing and this trail soon grew to a wider path. It appeared the people here regularly made their way to the stone chamber. A little too regularly, Nadia thought. "Aidan, what are we going to do if somebody spots us before we spot them?"

"Hmm, good point." After a brief discussion, the twins agreed walking down the well-worn path made for easy going, but left them too exposed. They decided to walk through the woods parallel to the trail and sacrifice some speed in favor of safety. This way, if they came across any of the local inhabitants, they hoped to see them first.

The thick bed of pine needles beneath their feet made it easy to travel in silence and the kids took turns in the lead as they walked steadily for an hour or more. A sudden squall forced them to stop briefly and huddle under the protective branches of a towering hemlock. The shower moved on as quickly as it had started and they were soon on their way again, breathing in the cool fresh air and the fragrance of green and growing things.

Aidan sat on a log for a moment to drink from a water bottle, then handed it to Nadia. He spoke softly, "It's so hard to tell exactly where we are without familiar landmarks, I don't even know how far we've walked."

"I know. Nothing looks the same. Uh, duh. 1500 years might make some changes, huh?" Nadia grinned and then crept through the trees to make sure they had not strayed too far away from the main trail. "So far, so good," she whispered. They stowed their water bottle, rechecked the compass, and pressed on toward the river.

With Aidan now in the lead, they continued shadowing the main trail. The going was faster now that the forest had opened up a bit, but with increased speed came reduced caution. Aidan's left foot found a dry dead branch and as his weight came down on it, it snapped with a pop like a gunshot.

A deep low growling grunt froze them in their tracks.

Then they saw it. Directly ahead of them, a mere twenty yards away was an enormous, black, angry bear and it was staring right at them. As the bear let out yet another even louder roaring grunt, two small cubs scrambled up a nearby birch tree. The mother bear began to swing her head slowly from side to side, testing the air with her nose. She then let out a long churning roar that culminated in a terrifying pop as she snapped her mouth shut, hard. Nadia's heart stopped and the cold chill of terror ran down her spine. She moaned.

Aidan whispered frantically to her. "Don't run. Be very still."

Nadia didn't think she could make her legs move even if she wanted to run. The fear filled her so completely she could hardly breathe.

The bear rose up on its hind legs and stood towering for a moment. Then, still roaring, it dropped to all fours and thundered straight at them. Before Nadia could draw a breath, she saw a movement to her right. From behind a giant birch tree, an Indian woman appeared, tall, regal and beautiful. She moved with grace and speed, stopping directly between the twins and the bear. Facing the bear, she held up her hand, palm outward and spoke softly and calmly to it. The twins did not recognize the language she spoke. However soft and calm her words were, they were clearly words of authority.

At the sound of the woman's voice, the mother bear pulled up suddenly and stopped. It took deep slow breaths as if willing itself to calm down and it studied the Indian woman with penetrating eyes. Again, the woman spoke and again the words were soft and calm, yet commanding.

Nadia couldn't believe her eyes. This woman stepped in front of a charging bear and wasn't at all afraid! Nadia could sense compassion and kindness, even love. But not fear. Like a guardian angel, clothed in cream-colored deerskin, she stood, tranquil and sure, in front of them, protecting them from the mother bear's wrath.

The bear stood stock still for a moment as if contemplating the woman's words, then turned, grunted softly to her cubs, then ambled off into the forest. The cubs slid down the tree and looked for just an instant with teddy bear faces and blinking eyes at the disbelieving twins, then scampered after their mother.

The woman turned to face them. Although she was not smiling, her gentle face held warmth and kindness.

Still reeling from the shock and terror, Nadia's breathing was ragged. "Thank you, thank you, thank you. How... how did you do that? It was coming straight at us – I couldn't move, we would have been killed." She brushed away the tears rolling down her cheeks and struggled to regain her composure.

Aidan put an arm around her shoulder and gave her a squeeze. He spoke to the lovely Indian woman, standing quietly before them. "Thank you... That was... um... thank you. Do you speak English?" He instantly felt like a fool for asking. How could she possibly know English? No English-speaking person arrived on this continent until the 1600s. He shook his head, irritated with himself, but the shock of the bear had unsettled him, too.

A feeling more than a sound drew the twins' attention as a raven threaded through the canopy above and rode the gentle breeze, on outstretched wings, across the clearing. In spite of its size, it landed delicately on the woman's shoulder. She reached up reflexively to run her fingers through its feathers and stroke its shiny black wing. The stately bird lifted its head and called out its gravelly cry, "Graa, graa." As it tipped back its head, Aidan could clearly see a splotch of white under its chin. This bird looked just like the raven from the attic and from Mystery Hill.

"Uh... Aidan, that sure looks like our raven," murmured Nadia.

"It sure does. And you know what that means... it means we are in the right place."

Nadia felt her heart lift in hope.

The Indian woman lifted her hand and when she spoke, it was in a lilting, melodic language. Her voice trailed up as she ended, as if she asked a question. Nadia shook her head. "I'm sorry, we don't understand you..."

The woman thought for a moment, then spoke again, clearly in a different language this time and again asking a question, but no more comprehensible than before. Once again, Nadia shook her head, her frustration mounting. She muttered to her brother, "If we can't communicate with anyone here how in the world are we going to find Conall?"

At that, the Indian woman's eyes opened wide. She repeated slowly and clearly, "Conall?"

"Yes!" Aidan nodded vigorously. "Conall. We are here to see Conall."

The woman nodded. She stood quietly for a moment studying the twins. Then, she appeared to make up her mind and gestured for them to follow her. With a soft smile, she turned to lead them along the well-traveled path toward the west. The raven lifted off her shoulder, pumped its ebony wings and melted into the shadows ahead.

Chapter 18

---◈---

"I feel like we've been walking for hours." Aidan said. "We can't be more than a mile or two from the spot where our house will be – someday, but... "

He didn't have to say it. Nadia knew he felt lost. This valley was so vast. While they did not know exactly where the Indian woman was taking them, they were still headed west. Aidan had been right about that, Nadia thought. The beautiful and mysterious woman had not turned nor spoken to them again, but walked noiselessly before them as they followed, sometimes struggling to keep up. Nadia marveled; she never seems to hurry, but she covers ground with amazing speed.

Finally, they reached the top of a rise and a wide grassy meadow stretched out before them, with an expanse of water beyond. The rainclouds had given way and there was the Hudson River sparkling in the sunshine with the outline of Storm King Mountain rising up from the opposite shore. They had grown up looking at that view and it was as familiar to them as an old friend.

Between the grassy slope and the river stood a small but bustling settlement, bisected by the road they were on. Nadia touched her brother's arm and he turned to her. This must be where they were headed.

"Amazing!" Aidan whispered, with a huge smile.

"I know," she replied. "I keep pinching myself..."

As they approached the village, Nadia could see it was organized into a very large loose circle, perhaps the length of two football fields in diameter. The perimeter consisted of a long sweeping arc of lodges. Each lodge was constructed of large slabs of bark attached to a framework of saplings.

"Great craftsmanship," Aidan said softly to Nadia.

Far from crude, these were substantial structures designed to withstand the elements, including the often-cruel Hudson Valley winters.

The area in the village center was an open space like a green or a common, surrounded by a random collection of small structures that resembled sheds or lean-tos. Laced between all of these were well-worn paths or avenues and small groups of Native American villagers congregated here and there, taking part in various activities.

Nadia asked Aidan quietly, "Algonquin?"

Aidan shrugged. "Hard to tell..."

Nadia watched young men and boys taking fish from baskets and hanging them on racks to dry in the sun. What fish were those? Perhaps Shad. The Shad Festival took place every year along the Hudson River and she wondered if these people also celebrated that silly-looking little fish.

Suddenly, her mouth watered at the thought of the hot, salty fish and chips they had at Georgina's Tavern, one of their favorite local restaurants. But, it would be 1500 years before there would be a Georgina's Tavern here. It was hard to wrap your brain around, Nadia thought.

As they followed the Indian woman into the center of the village, Nadia wondered what kind of reception they would get from these people. Would they be friendly? Would they search her and Aidan and take the Ravenstone? If so, how would they get back without it?

Stop it, Nadia, she said to herself. Just trust. The old man would not have sent them back if they couldn't return. Would he?

They walked on, passing another area where bear, deer, and other animal hides were stretched out in the sun, drying. They saw several Indian men and women building a canoe out of birch bark fastened over a frame of timber saplings. This village certainly was a busy place, she thought. But, as they passed, adults and children alike stopped what they were doing to stare.

The Indian woman was kind and Nadia sensed no ill will from her, but now, feeling them gaping at her, Nadia's heart started pounding again. She thought she and her brother must look like space aliens to these people. Her red T-shirt, cut off jeans, sneakers, and bright blue backpack stood out in glaring contrast to the deerskin-clad Indians. On this warm summer day, the men wore deerskin loincloths or breeches and the women were clad in simple dresses made of the same soft skin. Many of the villagers were barefoot.

She tried a hesitant smile toward a small group, but there was no response. She did not feel the same flood of kindness and warmth from these people that she'd felt from the

Indian woman. She recognized fear, wonder, even awe, plus some defensiveness. Not a good mix, she thought.

"Nadia, hang on a minute." Aidan nodded to his left. "I think you have an admirer."

Nadia turned to follow Aidan's gaze and came face-to-face with an Indian boy about their age, perhaps a little older. Like his neighbors around him, he was curious about the odd-looking strangers being led into the village. But, unlike the others, he was smiling. And he was smiling at Nadia.

"Never underestimate the power of a beautiful girl," Aidan said.

"Good grief," said Nadia. She rolled her eyes, shook her head and turned her head to hide her grin from her brother. But, with a final glance back, she saw more than the young boy grinning. Standing nearby were several villagers, staring after them. And they were not smiling.

At the northern tip of the village stood a lodge that was much larger, at least two or three times the size of the others. Approaching it, the shape of the gray bark-covered structure reminded Nadia of a blimp or a capsized ship.

She followed the Indian woman through the open doorway of the lodge and gazed around. The floor, dug perhaps a foot deep into the ground, made the structure look and feel much larger within than it appeared from the outside. An elevated platform stretched the length of the building against the outside walls. Ladders provided access to this platform, which appeared to provide bunks or beds.

At the front of the big main room stood a single large chair constructed of hewn wood and leather. The dirt floors were covered with rush mats and a pile of hides was stacked near the chair. One big bear skin, with bear's head intact, lay in front of the chair and Nadia felt her blood run cold as she stared at its enormous teeth. She shuddered; the brave Indian woman had certainly saved their lives.

The sound of the woman's voice broke the silence and the twins turned to face her. She pressed her hands against her chest and said, "Miakoda." She patted her chest and repeated, "Miakoda."

"Ah," said Aidan, nodding. He pointed to her. "You are Miakoda?" He smiled when she nodded in return and he clapped his hands to his chest. "Aidan," he said.

She nodded and tried it out. "Aidan."

The kids nodded vigorously and they repeated this with Nadia.

Miakoda pulled a couple of animal hides off the pile near the chair and gestured for them to sit. Crossing over to the wall, she pulled two long brown strips from a large basket and brought them over to them. Then she quietly disappeared out of the open door.

Aidan turned the strips over and over, examining them closely like a scientific specimen. Finally, he sniffed one, then cautiously bit off a piece. "Hey, it tastes just like beef jerky. Probably venison, though. It's good. Try it."

Nadia was too excited and nervous to be interested in dried mystery meat. "When are we going to find Conall? Do you think she's gone to get him?"

"Let's hope. And let's face it, things are going pretty well. The Indian woman was nice to us, she gave us something to eat..." As he chewed, Aidan turned in a long slow circle, his eyes rolling over every object in the lodge. "And we're getting a personal tour of history that scientists and archaeologists can only dream of. I can't believe I didn't bring my cell phone. I just kept thinking it wouldn't work here, of course. But, seriously, the pictures I could have taken!"

Nadia headed for the door, saying over her shoulder, "I'm going to poke around outside. I can't just sit here!"

"Ok, wait, I'll come with you, we need to stay together," Aidan said as he hurried to follow her.

Nadia only made it a few steps from the doorway of the lodge, when a powerful looking Indian stepped silently across her path, blocking her way. Dressed in deerskin breeches and moccasins, with feathers hanging from his long braid, he looked fierce, proud and determined.

As she stepped around him, he grabbed her firmly by the arm and spoke sharply in his own tongue. Nadia tried to pull free, but she was held fast. A grizzled old Indian woman rushed over wagging her finger at Nadia, scolding her in their unintelligible language.

"Hey, what are you doing, let her go!" Aidan shouted as he rushed to help free Nadia from the man's grasp. But, two more men had approached. They were tall, strong European-looking men dressed in tunics and breeches. They easily overpowered the twins and marched them, unceremoniously, back into the lodge, ignoring the kids' protests. Nadia's mouth went dry and she suppressed a shiver. She would not show her fear, she said to herself firmly, she would *not*.

There were huge daggers hanging, sheathed but ominous, from the men's belts. Suppressing her fear became more and more difficult, especially when she saw Aidan eying the daggers as well. As she watched him struggle even harder, she sensed his frustration and fear.

The twins were no match for the warriors and struggling was useless. The men bound Nadia and Aidan's hands behind their backs with rawhide straps then shoved the kids down onto the rugs in front of the single chair. Nadia landed face-to-face with the enormous teeth of the bear head.

Then, the men abruptly left the lodge, but through the open door, Nadia could see the Indian brave who had first grabbed her. He stood quietly staring at them and Nadia felt a sense of his distrust, yet wary curiosity. The bottom line was clear: he was posted to see the twins did not escape.

Aidan sighed. "Guess I spoke too soon about things going pretty well."

Although her arms and wrists ached, Nadia fell asleep where she had propped herself up against a wall. The fear had worn her down. As Nadia discovered, you could only maintain a fever pitch of stress or emotion for so long. Eventually, your body just knocked you out. Curled on the rug, his head resting on the bear head, Aidan, too, was drifting in and out of uncomfortable slumber.

As the late afternoon sun cast long shadows across the lodge floor, the twins were suddenly jolted wide-awake. A tall, regal-looking man entered the lodge, followed closely by Miakoda and a younger man, who appeared to be sixteen or seventeen years old. The twins struggled to their feet, which wasn't easy with their hands still bound behind them.

They had to communicate, somehow, Nadia thought. They had to get free, and they had to find Conall.

The tall man led the others the length of the room stopping directly in front of the twins. Nadia, her heart pounding, stared at the threesome before them. With pale skin and dressed in tunics, breeches, and boots, the two men looked like the men that had tied their hands; neither was Native American.

The older man, tall, strong and in the prime of his life, was clearly a leader. Movie star handsome, Nadia thought. With his wavy, black hair, and piercing blue eyes, he appeared to be of the same Black Irish stock that was present throughout her own family tree.

Yet, it was more than simply this man's physical appearance that commanded attention. The power of his presence somehow filled the room. Nadia tried to get a sense of his mood or feelings, but there was an impenetrable wall around him.

She was determined not to be intimidated – after all, the old man had sent them!

Then suddenly she *knew*. Nadia took a deep breath and stiffened her shoulders. Holding his gaze, in a clear strong voice she stated, "You are Conall."

The man did not reply, but continued to regard her with his piercing, deep blue eyes. The young man behind him stepped forward, his eyes wide. Fair-skin, auburn hair and short beard, he seemed to be about Heather's age, but he sure wasn't like any of the high school kids Nadia knew back in Cold Spring. He projected a level of seriousness and maturity, but also excitement, Nadia thought.

The young man spoke. "You speak English!"

"Thank God! You understand us – awesome!" Aidan burst out. "I am Aidan and this is my sister, Nadia." He stopped himself abruptly.

The young man gave a brief nod of his head. "My name is Patrick." He looked them up and down. "Where have you come from?"

Nadia said, "We have traveled a long way. To see Conall." She looked at the older man and when he did not respond, she glanced at her brother.

Aidan said, "We were sent..."

"You were sent?" Patrick glanced at the leader, who neither spoke nor moved, but continued to study them.

Nadia took over. "A wise shaman sent us here."

The flap of wings and a sharp "graa" broke the spell and they all turned to see the raven glide the length of the lodge. It floated softly past Patrick, Miakoda, and the older man, and came to rest, gently, on Aidan's shoulder.

Startled, Aidan's eyes grew wide and Nadia mouthed an involuntary, "Wow." There the great bird sat, quiet and regal, on his shoulder, while Nadia struggled to contain her excitement.

Miakoda reached for the older man's arm and spoke to him softly, in the melodic tongue the twins had heard before on Ninham Mountain.

Then, Patrick spoke again, to the twins. "Miakoda tells us that the raven took her to the forest today to meet you."

The kids stared at Miakoda. Silence held for a moment, then the older man gestured to Patrick to free them and waited as the kids' restraints were loosened. Nadia rubbed at the places on her wrist that had been chafed raw by the leather tie.

"Why have you come?" the older man asked in a deep, rich voice, a voice that held command.

Aidan shouted, "You speak English!"

Patrick explained. "He speaks the language spoken by anyone near him."

In her surprise and excitement, Nadia spoke without thinking. "You are Conall! Sir, we were sent to find you – we need your help!"

"Nadia." Aidan's voice held a warning tone.

She turned to him quickly, but spoke softly. "The old man told us, 'Seek Conall.'"

"But," Aidan whispered, "we don't know–" He stopped abruptly.

Nadia realized he was uncomfortable being unable to speak openly. But, she was sure that these people were their friends. "Trust me, Aidan. I know."

Aidan met her eyes, then slowly said, "You're right. The raven has cleared the way." He reached up to touch the huge bird gently and it responded with a soft, "Graa."

Patrick said, "The raven seems to know you."

Aidan nodded. "What we are about to tell you will sound unbelievable," he began. "We traveled here from the future – a long way into the future – in search of a special plant. This plant heals the sick and it is needed in our time. Our father is a scientist searching for a cure –"

Conall held up his hand, cutting Aidan off, and turned to Patrick, who directed his next words to Conall and Miakoda.

"A scientist is someone who studies the world through observation and experiment," Patrick explained. He turned back to the kids. "I take it your father is a doctor?"

The twins nodded and Nadia continued with their tale. "A wise old man appeared to us in a mirror –"

Once again, Patrick had to explain to Conall. Of course, thought Nadia, there were no mirrors in 459!

"A mirror is a thing that lets you see your own reflection." Patrick thought for a moment. "Very like looking down into a still lake."

Conall spoke softly in yet another language, to Miakoda. Obviously, he was sharing this with her, thought Nadia, and the woman smiled gently at the kids. Nadia met the lovely Indian woman's eyes and felt herself relax. It was as if her mom had given her a hug. Maybe everything was going to be all right.

Aidan addressed the three people standing before them, "The plant we are looking for looks like a black fern. We need to take it back to our time..." His voice trailed off.

"By using the black Ravenstone." Conall was not asking, he spoke surely and calmly. He strode over to the wall behind the large chair, grabbed the corner of an intricate silk tapestry and calmly pulled it away. There, on the wall beneath it, was an exquisitely decorated shield. It was approximately two feet in diameter, with a large black raven engraved in the center. Mounted on the shield's entire outer edge were eight black stones. And a wreath of Celtic knot design encircled the central image of the raven.

As beautiful and impressive as the shield was, what captured the twins' attention was the fact that the shield was glowing. Just as the Ravenstone glowed in the doorway of the chamber, the shield pulsed with light as though it had a life of its own.

Chapter 19

---◆---

"You traveled through the doorway of the stone chamber," said Conall.

Nadia pulled her eyes away from the glowing shield on the wall. It was mesmerizingly beautiful, a work of art. And it clearly held power and magic.

Aidan asked, "How do you know that we– " His eyes widened. "Oh. If you know about the stone and the chamber..." He stopped.

Conall sat down in the chair under the shield and motioned for them to sit, as well. "I created the Ravenstone." He paused, then looked away, lost in thought.

The kids stood stunned, silenced, staring at Conall.

Then, Patrick picked up with the story. "It was created with the help of the greatest shaman leader in Iar Connacht, in the north-western corner of Ireland. Conall and his brother Kane carved it from the black basalt stone of the Giant's Causeway."

Conall turned back to the two young people before him. "So yes, Aidan and Nadia, I know of the Ravenstone. And now, what you must know is that it is not safe here. It was sent to the future for a reason and must go back. I know you have it with you in the bag on your back."

Aidan hesitated, then reached into his pack and pulled out the stone. Like the nearby shield hanging on the wall, the Ravenstone was glowing red and gold, pulsing slowly.

"It speaks to the shield. They are of one mind." Conall stood, pointing at the stone. "But it must leave this time and place and soon. Or it will bring great danger."

Nadia's heart started to race. Now what? Just when she thought everything was going to work out. "What... great danger?" She spoke tentatively, still unsure of her place conversing with this great man. He *created* the Ravenstone! She could only imagine the power he must hold.

"Give the stone to me," demanded Conall. The command in his voice was impossible to ignore and Aidan found he had taken a step toward him before he even thought, or could respond. He stopped himself abruptly.

Nadia felt the fear course through her and she knew Aidan felt it too. How could they just hand over the Ravenstone? After all, it was their only way to get home! To ever see their mom and dad again!

As Conall stood with his hand outstretched for the stone, Patrick said quickly, "It will be safer with Conall."

Conall spoke again, more gently this time. "We desire the same thing, young Aidan, for you to go home to your time and take the stone with you. We will lead you to the powerful healing herb you call the Black Fern. But until we do, the stone is safer with me. If you keep it, there will be great risk."

Patrick added, "Believe me, no one would dare try to take it from Conall."

Nadia's moment of fear passed and she slowly began to accept the wisdom of their words. She took a deep breath, studied Conall and began to experience calm acceptance and a true sense of the older man's goodwill.

Locking eyes with Aidan, she nodded. Her brother studied her for a moment, then, as if he sensed her thoughts and agreed on some unspoken level, he slowly placed the black stone in Conall's hand. The twins watched as the older man slipped it into a pouch inside his tunic. Aidan's eyes lingered on the pouch. And on the man they had traveled so far to meet.

Nadia heard her twin brother's thoughts as if he had spoken them aloud. *I hope this does not come back to haunt me,* she heard. Placing their trust in someone they didn't know was huge. This must be to do with my ability to read people, she thought. Is that power growing? And was it somehow thanks to the Ravenstone? In any event, I hope this is not one of the times I am wrong, she thought with a shudder.

Nadia was stuffed. She didn't think she'd ever eaten so much meat at one time in her life. But oh, my, was it ever delicious! Elk meat, which Patrick, Conall, and the other village hunters had brought home today was roasted over an open fire. If she felt full, how must Aidan feel? He'd eaten twice what she had! But then, Mom always said he had a hollow leg.

Most of the villagers, it seemed, had finally begun to accept the presence of the twins. As odd as we must look to them, Nadia thought, we're just kids. Also, sitting with Patrick, Miakoda, and Conall makes us acceptable, if not understandable.

Many of the Indians had gone to their lodges for the night, others sat in groups nearby, or on the other side of the huge fire pit, talking, relaxing, and munching on dried berries. But, from time to time throughout the evening, they would turn to stare again, warily, at the intruders in their strange clothes.

Nadia leaned back on her elbows on a deerskin hide under her and gazed up at the starry sky. Silvery smoke from the waning fire curled upward, creating feathery swirls that disappeared into the stars. And what stars! She had never seen so many stars, so brilliant and clear, a sparkling multitude across the night sky. The stars did not have to compete with artificial light from the Earth; there were no cities with skyscrapers surrounded by acres of illuminated parking lots, connected by ribbons of highway. There was nothing. Light from electricity had not been invented yet!

What a day it had been. She could hardly believe that twelve short hours ago she'd been eating breakfast with Nana Jean in New Hampshire. It felt like a million miles and a lifetime ago. Nadia shook her head slightly, in amazement.

"I will now tell you my story." Patrick's voice brought Nadia back from her contemplations and she sat up to listen and focus. She and Aidan were eager to learn who Patrick was, where he was from and how exactly an English-speaking teenager ended up in the Hudson Valley a hundred years before Henry Hudson sailed up the river. Why was an Irish shaman living here in the Hudson Valley? And what was the "great danger" Conall had spoken of? Although, Nadia hated to add the chill of fear to this beautiful June evening.

The twins had bombarded Patrick with these questions, but he had just said, "Later, I will explain everything, later." Instead, during the feast, the twins had learned more about Conall and Mia. They were highly revered in the village and Conall was, in fact, the leader of this small tribe, even though he was not Native American. Miakoda, too, was held in high regard as the daughter of a great Wappinger chief and "Queen" of this village.

They'd also learned that far from being a surprise, the arrival of the twins was somehow expected. Conall had turned the hunting party back to the village early. When Patrick had asked him why, Conall's brief reply was, "Great change is upon us. The shield is calling to me. We must return at once."

Patrick began to speak, slowly, as if wondering where to start. "Conall is as a father to me." Nadia and Aidan waited expectantly. Patrick looked around, ensuring there were no villagers within earshot and said, softly, "I too know of the stone, I time-traveled with it four years ago." He gazed into the fire, his eyes far away. "My twin sister and I found the stone. The time-travel was an accident. I wanted so much to see where the stone was created, to be there during that time! We were torn apart during the golden arc of light and sound."

"You've never seen her again," Nadia said gently. Patrick shook his head. Nadia simply could not imagine never seeing Aidan again.

Patrick went on. "I was thrown back in time, but also across space. I found myself in northwestern Ireland, where Conall took me in. He and his twin brother, Kane, are the sons of a great chieftain there. Conall is only a few minutes older than Kane, but as the first-born, he is next in line and is the favored son of the chieftain. It was obvious Kane was not happy with this situation, was not content to sit on the sidelines. There is much bad blood between them."

Aidan asked, "Kane is still in Ireland?"

When Patrick nodded, Nadia asked the question the twins had been wondering. "How did you and Conall get here?"

"The stone." Patrick's small smile was almost rueful. "It is all about the stone – what do you call it? The Ravenstone? That is perfect. Yes, we traveled with the Ravenstone. As I am sure you are aware, only twins can use the stone."

The kids nodded. They'd worked this out, but it was good to have it confirmed.

"Conall had... has... two nephews who are also identical twins. Those young kids brought us – six of us, all touching the shoulders or arms of the kids. We traveled together, from Connacht to the stone chamber on Ninham Mountain, the same chamber through which I had traveled to Ireland. I told Conall of this tunnel through time and space and he chose it as the place to come, to hide the stone from Kane."

There was a pause while the twins digested this. Then Nadia ventured a hesitant, "Why?"

The twins watched as Patrick absentmindedly tossed some bits of meat to the two dogs hovering nearby. The kids waited. Nadia curbed her eagerness, her impatience, to let him tell his tale. Things clearly moved at a slower pace in 459. She must honor that.

Patrick said, "The stone is imbued with many powers, some intentional and some not. We learned it magnifies the user's greatest skills and character traits. If a twin has the gift of precognition, using the stone will enhance that power." He paused and as he thought, he rubbed his fingers through his short auburn-colored beard. "As for character traits, if one uses the stone with honor and courage, he will become more honorable and more courageous. Do you see?"

Nadia smiled and bowed her head in agreement. She turned to her brother. "You wondered if our intuition, our ability to read people, was growing – like how you got emotion from Aunty-Gran at the stone chamber?

Aidan nodded.

"Well, it's not my imagination." she said. "It's much stronger now," she said. "The power is growing."

"Yes, it is." Aidan agreed, "I feel it too."

Patrick nodded. "It is the power of the Ravenstone. The more you use it, the greater your skills will become."

Aidan and Nadia glanced at each other. She could read and feel her brother's thoughts from time to time. But today it happened over and over again. Many times he had spoken exactly what she was thinking. Or, she had somehow managed to hear what he had not said.

Patrick continued. "Conall is a good and noble man. He has many great skills and talents, all of which the Ravenstone amplified. He is kind, brave, and full of honor. Those traits are heightened by the stone, as is his great capacity for healing." Patrick stopped, and gazed into the fire, absentmindedly popping a few berries into his mouth. Then he continued, "Unfortunately, Conall's brother Kane does not share his good and noble traits. His lifelong jealousy of Conall fuelled his way down a dark path. Kane has chosen greed and love of power and is utterly insensitive to other people's desires or feelings. He is dangerously and cruelly self-centered."

Suddenly, from off to the right, a wolf's howl rent the air and Nadia jumped. It was mournful and haunting and sounded very close. She quickly looked over at Patrick, who seemed unconcerned. Even when a second wolf howled an answer and Patrick noticed Nadia's shocked expression, his voice was mild and calm.

"They will never bother us here," he said.

"The fire, right?" asked Aidan.

Patrick nodded. "The fire, the people, our own dogs..."

He reached down to the ground for a gourd full of water, drank, and placed it back on the ground beside him. "Let me tell you an ancient Indian legend. Inside each of us, there wages a terrible battle between two wolves. One wolf is evil, full of greed, superiority, and ego. The other wolf is of goodness, kindness, courage, honor. Which wolf is it that wins the war inside each one of us?" He looked over at Nadia and Aidan, listening intently. "The one that you feed."

Nadia said, "And Kane feeds the evil wolf?"

Patrick sighed. "Kane has become the evil wolf. So, you can see, he must never possess the Ravenstone."

Nadia shivered.

Aidan said, "And Kane is the great danger that Conall was talking about."

Patrick nodded again. "That's right, Aidan. In the beginning, Conall and the great Irish shaman believed they could handle or control Kane in some way, appeal to his better self. Sadly, over time, Conall came to realize there was no longer a better self in his twin. He struggled with this for some time and finally decided he must remove the Ravenstone from his brother's reach."

"Why not just destroy it?" Aidan asked.

"Conall could not bring himself to destroy a tool with such potential for good. But he had to keep it away from Kane – if he ever got it he would be unstoppable Once we arrived here, near the River that Flows Both Ways, Conall concluded that the Ravenstone had to be sent where Kane could never reach it. The twins who led us here from Ireland volunteered to use the stone chamber, one more time, to take the Ravenstone one hundred years into the future. Conall hoped mankind of the future would be more able to use the Ravenstone for the benefit of all."

Nadia realized she was chewing on her thumbnail and yanked her hand away from her mouth.

Miakoda approached and spoke with Patrick in her soft language, then waved goodnight and disappeared into the lodge. Conall remained outside, standing alone a ways off from the fire pit, staring up at the sky. Nadia watched him, quietly, for a few moments. His guard must be down, she thought, for now she could sense his mood, his emotions. He seemed burdened by a sense of grimness and sadness. She couldn't possibly know the thoughts weighing heavily on a prince, a great shaman. But, with all she had just learned, she now suspected that the source of his concern was his brother, Kane.

She asked Patrick, "But Kane is a long way away, isn't he? He's across the ocean in Ireland? How can he be a danger to us, here?"

"Conall assumes he is still in Ireland, yes. But, he will see and feel the Ravenstone's presence in our time. You see, Kane, too, possesses a shield, the mirror image of the one you saw glowing in Conall's lodge. It will have come alive the moment you arrived at the stone chamber this morning. Kane will be unable to resist it and he will be on his way. It is only a matter of time."

Nadia shivered.

Patrick reached down for another handful of dried red berries and offered some to the kids. They munched for a few moments.

"You see," Patrick continued, "the stones around the edge of the shield are like the points of a compass. They glow when the shield senses the presence of the Ravenstone. If the Ravenstone lies to the east, the stone pointing to the east on the shield will glow and pulse. If the Ravenstone remains in our time, Kane will eventually follow the shield right to this village."

"Won't it take him a month to cross the ocean... at least?" Aidan asked. "As soon as we can get the Black Fern we'll be back in the 21st century, safe and sound." He looked over at Nadia and they both smiled in relief.

Patrick nodded. "Yes, you're right. We just need to get you home... safe and sound."

"It must have been hard for Conall to part with the Ravenstone," Nadia said.

"Doing what is right is often difficult, doing it anyway is what great men do," was Patrick's wise reply.

Aidan nodded. "And what about the twins that took the Ravenstone into the future? What happened to them?"

"We have no idea. That's a source of enormous grief for Conall, although he balances that grief with the honor and respect he carries in his heart for them. They gave a gift of great service." Patrick paused and looked down at his hands. "They were about your age. We pray they are well and enjoying lives in a future time."

Nadia couldn't imagine being torn from her home and time, never to return. "As for you, Patrick, you were alone in a strange time and did not have the Ravenstone. Or your twin sister. Right?"

"Right. When I last saw my sister, the Ravenstone was still in her hand."

Nadia said, "So, you couldn't return to your time. What year was it when you traveled with the stone – you said it was four years ago?"

"Yes, it was 1892... my 13th birthday," Patrick said. "I assure you I am at peace with the knowledge that I am where I belong. Conall is instructing me in shamanic tradition and healing. It is my path, I knew it from the beginning and I am more sure every day. But, I do worry about my twin sister. She never knew what became of me. I miss Nora and I wonder – "

"Nora?!" Nadia spoke too loudly in her surprise and several Indians nearby stopped their conversation and looked over at her. "Nora?" she repeated, softly.

Patrick's eyes widened and his eyebrows lifted.

The twins spoke at the same moment. "Patrick and Nora!" They stared at each other.

Then Aidan threw back his head and laughed. "You are Patrick, who was lost on Ninham Mountain more than a hundred years ago! You are Nora's brother – she was our great, great grandmother!"

Patrick's jaw dropped.

Nadia said, "We are related to you, Patrick! No one ever knew what happened to you!"

**Hudson Highlands, Ninham Mountain,
and the Hudson River 459 A.D.**

Chapter 20

———◆———

The soft morning light dappled the forest floor as the twins followed Mia and Patrick along the same woodland trail that had brought them to the village. They quickly veered off the main trail and headed south, wending their way through the unspoiled woods and occasional clearings. The air was warm and sweet and Nadia marveled at the pure sounds of nature. There were no planes flying overhead, no distant sounds of traffic whining along the interstate. Only the birds, the breeze and the river competed for her attention.

The raven, like a sentinel, perched serenely on Patrick's shoulder. Occasionally it soared off to disappear into the woods, only to return a few minutes later, reclaiming his position on the young man's shoulder.

Although Nadia felt exhausted from lack of sleep, her mind was buzzing from all she'd learned, from all the new jigsaw-puzzle pieces of this mission. After falling quickly to sleep from sheer fatigue, she had woken in the middle of the night to the distant howling of wolves. It took a while for her heart to slow back down and then she struggled to sleep for the rest of the night. She'd heard Aidan, in the bunk directly below hers, tossing and turning as well.

Now, she noticed Aidan was yawning. "You didn't sleep much either, did you?" she asked.

"I kept waking up in a sweat."

"Why? It wasn't hot," said Nadia.

"No... Every time I fell asleep, I had this dream or vision. I kept seeing an ancient sailing ship under full sail. With a crew of armed men."

Nadia looked at him sharply.

"Swords, daggers, the whole nine yards," he said.

Nadia thought for a moment. "Must be your overactive imagination," she said softly.

"Not something you normally worry about with me, right?" His rueful smile was short-lived.

"Be serious, Aidan. I think it's just your mind driving you crazy. Since being clairvoyant is not one of your gifts, it had to be the thought that Kane might be on his way."

"Yeah," Aidan replied. "Good then, that we have an entire ocean between him and us, huh?"

Nadia nodded and they walked in silence for a few moments.

Then Aidan continued, "But I do hate that we don't have the Ravenstone. I felt better when we could get away. I always knew we had that escape. Now I feel powerless."

Patrick, up ahead on the path with Mia, paused to wait for Aidan and Nadia. He had been eager, last night, to hear all about his sister Nora and the twins had told him everything they knew: that she had become an artist of some renown with a loyal local following, she had married, raised a family, and lived in the same home for the rest of her life. She had died peacefully at the age of 82.

However, it was clear Nora had never uttered a word to anyone in all her years, about the Ravenstone, or about Patrick vanishing from her sight that horrible day. She must have kept the Ravenstone hidden and taken the secret to her grave.

"Hearing about Nora's wonderful life and accomplishments has amazed me and set my heart at ease," said Patrick, as he walked next to them through the woods. "I'm so relieved. For these past four years, I have had no idea what happened to her that day. You see, for all I knew, she was thrown into a different time and different place, just as I was. It haunted me that she could be lost in time and I was not there to help her."

That idea had not occurred to Nadia. As quickly as she fit each new piece into the puzzle, even more pieces appeared and the puzzle itself grew larger.

Patrick continued, "It must have been hard for Nora too, she must have been terrified when I disappeared. We were so very close. To spend the rest of her life wondering and never knowing what became of me..." He trailed off.

Nadia exclaimed, "She never told a soul. Isn't that amazing?"

They all grew silent, focusing on crossing a rocky little stream with mossy banks. The woods ahead opened slightly, broken by small clearings where grasses and wildflowers grew. They could hear the cooing of doves or pigeons that grew louder with every step they took. Nadia peered up into the trees and saw soft gray birds perched on many branches. Off to the east, the trees were so laden with birds the branches bowed and drooped.

Aidan's eyes followed his sister's gaze. "Beautiful, aren't they?"

She nodded. She was making a mental note to find out what kind of birds they were. They didn't look like mourning doves but they didn't look like the pigeons in New York City either. They looked like something in between. And there were so many of them.

"You want to know about the Black Fern, as you call it," said Patrick. "I only know it by its Indian name. It is a treasured and much-trusted healing plant. The Indians introduced it to us soon after we arrived here. I have seen fever, sepsis, and other conditions resolve quickly and completely with the use of this herb."

He explained that this plant was plentiful, but only grew in one location, on the woodland floor under a grove of birch trees. To reach the birch grove they crossed a large meadow, its wild native flowers bobbing gold and orange in the sunlight.

Reaching the far side of the meadow, they could see the delicate black fronds floating above the moss on the forest floor ahead of them. It was a veritable sea of black fern swaying gently in the morning breeze. Nadia had never seen anything like them.

Close up, the black plant was indeed a fern and it grew happily in shady woodland, as did others in the fern family. But it did not look like any fern Nadia had ever seen. Both the stems and the fronds were thick and fleshy and were covered with soft fuzz. The entire glen was filled with a tantalizing fragrance, which grew stronger when the plants were crushed.

Nadia knelt down beside a clump of the plants and plucked off a piece. She rolled the leaf gently between her palms as Mia had shown her. Then, bringing her cupped hands to her face, she breathed in the wonderful fragrance. It smelled like a cross between sugar cane and vanilla.

Perhaps it was only her imagination, she thought, but with the fragrance came a sense of well-being. It flooded through her and she looked up to grin at Aidan and Patrick.

"Mom is going to love this stuff." Nadia knew her naturopath mother would be thrilled to find a plant that offered such healing. Never mind the fact that Dad would be able to isolate the active chemical component and develop a drug that might save thousands of people worldwide. That, she mused, was the plan.

The twins had prepared for this moment, knowing they must carefully transport the plants as safely as possible, across time, to deliver them to their father. Aidan pulled out a padded manila envelope and several self-sealing plastic food bags from his pack. Mia watched in fascination. Transparent plastic bags? Even Patrick seemed captivated by these odd items from the future. As Nadia plucked the leaves, Aidan carefully wrapped them in paper towels he moistened in a small pond. Then, using his penknife, he dug down around three of the smaller plants and lifted them out of the moist soil, root and all. He wrapped the whole plants, with their roots, in damp paper towels and placed them in bags, as well.

As the kids finished stowing their precious cargo safely away in their backpacks, Nadia felt a sudden chill of dread run through her. She glanced over toward Mia and Patrick, who had moved further into the meadow and were busy collecting wildflowers in a pouch. Echinacea, she thought. She took a deep breath and there was a moment of great stillness. Why do I feel so uncomfortable?

Then everything seemed to happen at once. Turning to look at her brother, Nadia saw movement on the far side of the meadow. It was Conall. He must have decided to join them after all. The quiet moment was shattered by a loud shrieking "Graa" and Nadia watched as the huge raven lifted off Patrick's shoulder. Its enormous wings pumped as it clawed its way up into the sky and raced, still calling out, directly north toward the village.

"Conall!" Aidan turned back to face the tall black-haired figure across the meadow and he raised a hand in greeting. At the same instant, he heard Mia cry out, in her own language. She was waving her arms and shouting as she ran toward the kids.

Aidan took a step in Conall's direction, but suddenly a dozen men, armed with spears, plunged out of the woods near them and grabbed Aidan and Nadia, who struggled fiercely.

Her heart racing in her chest and terror filling her, Nadia whirled and shouted Patrick's name; he was desperately defending Mia and trying to keep the attackers at bay.

He was failing.

"She says that's not Conall, not her husband!" Patrick screamed over the noise and chaos.

The tall man, who looked just like Conall, began to stride across the meadow toward Mia. She spun around and broke free from the man who was holding her. Rushing to the center of the meadow, she raised her arms high above her head, gazing upward and calling out, in a commanding, clear voice. She whirled in a circle, her head thrown back to the sky, while she called again and again.

What on earth? Nadia's arms were tightly held behind her, as were Aidan's, held firmly by strange warriors in tunics and breeches. With swords or bows and arrows at the ready.

The tall man reached Mia as the man pursuing her caught up and they grabbed her and held her fast.

"Kane." The voice in her head was clear. Nadia knew the truth and in an instant, realized the dire nature of their predicament. She fought with all her might in a moment of true panic.

"*Run!*" It was Mia's voice, speaking in her native language, but Nadia understood her. "Run!" the Indian woman called again, then cried out as one of the tall Celtic men struck her.

Suddenly Nadia was aware of a sound that had started as a low and distant hum but was now all around them and growing in volume. It sounded as if a distant storm had overtaken them. The noise seemed to be coming from everywhere, swelling until it was deafening. The sky darkened and Nadia looked up into a gigantic cloud. No, no, not a cloud! It was a storm of birds casting a giant shadow over the entire meadow. The swirling mass of birds was descending like a winged vortex. Millions of birds flapping millions of wings.

Through her struggle and gasping for breath, Nadia realized what was happening. The beautiful dove-like birds they'd seen weighing down the trees had lifted off and answered Mia's calls. Thousands of them blotted out the sun and filled the sky with sound. They were swirling and swooping and diving as though of one mind, like a school of fish. And all the while, they were pecking and attacking the men who held them. She could not see Aidan or Mia. She could not see Patrick! All she could see was the dark shadow and all she could hear and feel was the rush of the wind from the countless beating wings.

Kane's men, stunned and terrified by this sudden onslaught from the unknown, this dark magic, released their captives and took to slashing at the sky with their spears and swords.

The twins rushed toward Patrick, who broke free and began to run northward. Through the din, more in her head than from her ears, Nadia heard Mia compel them... *Run! Run! Escape!*

"Run back and get Conall!" Patrick's cries were so determined, so commanding, the twins instantly began running north as well, for the wood line.

They heard Kane shouting, "The kids! The kids! Grab them! They're only birds, you fools, forget them! Grab the kids!"

Aidan turned and shouted to Patrick, "Mia! We can't leave her!" But he could not see her and Patrick grabbed his arm, shouting to him as he pulled him toward the trees.

"Run!" he screamed. "Kane has her! We must get Conall!"

Once shielded from view by the trees, Aidan stopped, dragging at Nadia's arm to get her to stop, too. He ducked down behind a huge fallen oak tree, hiding behind the root ball and trunk. Back at the scene in the meadow, the huge cloud of birds continued to blacken the sky as they tormented Kane and his men.

"Wait, they are not following us, Patrick!" he hissed. Patrick whipped around and dropped down beside them.

"Come, Aidan, there is nothing you can do!"

"Wait, Patrick. We can't just leave her! If only, if *only* we had the Ravenstone – oh, Nadia, we could have used it to free her, to save her!"

Nadia shook her head. "No, Aidan, no! We could never take a chance like that! We haven't done anything like that before. If anything went wrong..." her voice softened and slowed. "If anything went wrong, all this would have been for nothing. No, Patrick is right. Conall will know what to do – Come *on*!" She pulled at him.

"Your sister is right. Hurry!" Patrick jumped up from his crouch and loped off through the woods. Nadia yanked again at her brother's arm and he finally stood up.

Aidan gave one long backward glance toward the meadow behind him, then started after Patrick and Nadia, toward the village.

Chapter 21

———✦———

Nadia tried to focus, tried to think, as she raced back toward the village with Aidan and Patrick. She refused to allow tears. "We will solve this and get home safely. We must. But, how on earth could Kane be here? Conall and Patrick told us he was still in Ireland. She looked back for the hundredth time, terrified Kane's men might descend on them at any moment.

"I know," said Aidan. "I don't understand how he got here so fast or how he found us in the meadow. But I know what we have to do. We have to save Mia."

Nadia agreed. Somehow, they had to help Conall. After all, wasn't all this happening because they had arrived with the Ravenstone? Weren't they the reason Mia was now a captive? Her fear hardened into resolve. This was their fault and she was determined they would put it right. But how?

"You were born to this path! This quest is your fate."

She heard the voice of the wise old sage once more, in her head. Her heart lifted and she reminded herself, again, that they had been sent. They were not alone. There was a greater purpose at stake and they were allied with a force greater than themselves.

Have some faith, she thought to herself.

"The raven has brought Conall!" Patrick gestured ahead, as he shouted.

Up ahead, striding toward them, were Conall and a group of a dozen or so men. Three were his own Celtic guards, the rest were Native American men. All were armed, either with spears or bows and arrows, while Conall wore a wide, intricately carved scabbard, which held a heavy sword. Embedded in the sword's hilt, black stones caught the sunlight and sparkled as he walked.

The huge black raven soared overhead, chiding with his strange guttural "Graa," then swooped down to alight on Patrick's shoulder.

Conall and his men did not even slow their pace as they passed, and the twins and Patrick wheeled around to follow them, retracing their footsteps toward the meadow where they'd left Kane. Kane and Mia. Patrick strode alongside Conall and immediately began to speak in a language Aidan assumed was old Irish. He was clearly updating his leader. As Patrick spoke, Conall did not respond, and even when the young man was finished, Conall's face remained as if carved in stone.

Nadia found she had to jog to keep up with the small army of men. Her head was still spinning – how could this have happened? And what were they going to do? Could she and Aidan take the Ravenstone and go to the stone chamber, return to their own time and be safe? No, she thought, they could not leave Mia in the hands of Kane.

As they approached the edge of the meadow, Conall slowed while his men fanned out to either side of him, forming a battle line facing Kane. Patrick stood at Conall's right hand, with the twins close behind.

Kane sat perched on a large rock at the far edge of the meadow, chewing nonchalantly on a long stem of meadow grass. Nadia noted the malignant smile and silently compared Kane to Conall. She could just kick herself for having been fooled.

Mia still managed to look regal and proud, as two large men stood either side of her, gripping her arms firmly.

Kane briefly studied Conall from across the meadow, then stood and strolled a few paces into the knee deep grass, calling out, "Hail, my wayward brother! We thought we had lost you to the bottom of the sea!"

"You are a coward, Kane. To hold a helpless woman." Conall's deep voice rang out strong and sure.

"My dear Conall. 'Helpless woman?' I doubt that very much. She seems to have wily ways, not unlike those of her new husband. Yes, I hear congratulations are in order?"

"What do you want?" Conall barked.

"What, no small talk? Tsk tsk. And here I was expecting a nice, warm welcome. Still, never mind." Kane seemed abruptly to abandon his pretense of friendliness and family spirit. His voice hardened. "I come for the stone which you stole from me." As he spoke, more of Kane's men stepped forward from the trees, to flank him on either side.

"The stone is better off in other hands than yours, Kane," called Conall. "Besides, of what use is it to you? You must certainly know I will never help you use it. There is little we agree on and we will never hold the same passion in our minds or hearts. You are powerless to use the stone alone."

"But my dear Conall," replied Kane, "you've been gone from our shores for several years and a great deal has happened in your absence. Dear old Riordan, our great shaman mentor, has passed away. But, he was, uh, persuaded to tell me a great deal before he died. Such as the many powers of the stone, of which you know nothing. And where the stone had gone. I thought I would come pay you a visit and lo and behold, my shield began to glow. Led me right up the beautiful River Which Flows Both Ways. Things always did work out for me, wouldn't you say, my brother?"

Nadia whispered quickly to Conall, "Sir, he is lying about something."

"It is one of his unfailing characteristics," was Conall's curt reply. "But how can you know that?"

"She is often able to read what is in people's hearts and minds," Aidan explained. "And her power has grown since we used the stone." Conall nodded as Aidan continued quietly, "You should also know that one of Kane's men is missing, there are only 11 now... there were twelve."

Conall turned sharply to look at Aidan, his deep blue eyes intent. "You are sure?"

Nadia said softly, "He is. He has a photographic memory – I mean, sir, he can remember every detail of anything he has seen. Trust me, he knows."

Conall studied the twins, eyebrows raised for a moment, then turned back toward his brother, across the meadow.

He called out, "If you harm her I will kill you, brother or not. Set her free, Kane. Now. She is not a part of this. This is between you and me."

Kane replied, "Oh, yes, my dear brother, I am more than willing to give you what is yours..." Then he paused and let silence fill the spring air. "... in exchange for what is mine. Your lovely wife for the great black stone."

Nadia gasped. Oh, *no*. She could hardly breathe. There was a long tense stillness, broken only by the raven's "Graa" in the woods nearby.

She locked eyes with Aidan. He shook his head imperceptibly and she knew his thoughts: Conall would never do it. There would be another way.

"Think about it," called out Kane. He gestured with his arms, pointing all around him. "Think of this lovely land you have found, your new life, your new wife, your thriving little village. Is fighting over the stone worth it? You cannot win, brother." He paused. "I know you do not desire bloodshed. I am accompanied by 75 strong warriors – men who would gladly fight to the death for me."

Evil, darkness, lies. It flooded through Nadia and she quickly whispered to Conall, "Lies, sir. Not that many men and they do not fight out of loyalty, they fear him."

"He is stalling, sir," Patrick spoke. "If Aidan is right, then the missing man has probably gone to fetch the rest of Kane's men. He must have a ship anchored on the river. The rest of the crew could easily be another thirty or forty men. He is stalling, killing time until he has enough men to overpower us."

Kane shouted again from his position across the meadow. "You take your time, brother. You will see that I am right."

Conall said to the twins and Patrick, "Wait here."

Abruptly, he turned and strode into the woods, just out of sight. Patrick and the twins stared at each other, as several minutes passed.

When Conall reappeared, he shouted one word to his twin brother, Kane. "Agreed."

The twins gasped, but Conall continued as if they weren't there. "One condition: You will take the stone and leave immediately, back where you came from across the sea and never return to this land again."

Kane shouted, "But of course, dear Conall, of course! I wish you nothing but happiness here in your new life!"

Nadia, in her confusion and shock, stared at this evil man. Suddenly she envisioned Kane as a long black snake, with deep blue eyes, its long tongue curling across the meadow to touch them with its poison. She shuddered. A nightmare, she thought. I am in a nightmare. I will wake up and all of this will have been a horrible dream.

"Sir, Conall, there must be another way. You can't give him the stone." Aidan's voice was urgent, desperate, pleading. "Let me and Nadia use it to free her – there must be something else we can do! Sir, you can't give him the stone!"

As if Aidan had not spoken, Conall turned to Liam, one of his right-hand men. He reached into his tunic and withdrew the black stone with raven heads at either end. "Bring him the stone, my friend. Make the exchange."

Liam nodded, bowed his head slightly to Conall and turning, he began to stride toward the middle of the meadow.

"No!" shouted Aidan and he moved to go after Liam.

Patrick reached for him, holding him by the arm. "No Aidan, you can't interfere – leave this to Conall!"

"Bring my wife into the meadow, Kane. Now." Conall's voice was hard, cold and commanding.

Kane nodded in compliance and he gestured to one of his men, who began to lead Mia across the meadow, toward Liam.

Time seemed to stand still for the brief minutes it took the three to meet. It felt like a lifetime to Nadia, standing at the edge of the meadow in the shadows of the white birch trees. Her hands were over her mouth and she had to remind herself to breathe.

Kane shouted from the edge of the meadow, "No tricks – show me the stone!"

Liam held the shining black stone high above his head and turned it from side to side so Kane could see it.

Nadia's eyes widened. Sensations flooded through her from Kane: greed, desire, and obsession, directed toward the black stone as it came nearer and nearer. Nadia drew in a long breath, waiting, hoping, praying...

The two men slowed as they reached the middle of the large meadow. Kane's man reached out for the stone, but Liam held it fast.

"Release her!" shouted Conall from his position at the edge of the meadow. Kane's man studied the stone, then turned, still gripping Mia and nodded to Kane.

At Kane's signal, he loosened his grip on Mia's arm and she slid past Liam, on her way back across the meadow toward Conall and her people.

Liam released the stone, never breaking eye contact with Kane's henchman, then turned abruptly on his heel to follow Mia.

Kane's guard, gripping the stone, marched back toward his leader. Overcome by his desire to feel and hold the stone once more, Kane strode the last few paces to close the gap and grabbed the black stone from the man's outstretched hand. With a look that bordered on madness, Kane let out a great cry of victory as he stared at the prize he held so tightly in his hands.

But, his joy was short-lived. His look of victory changed to confusion. Before his disbelieving eyes the great stone, the focus of his obsession, began to move. It twisted and turned, swelling and shifting. The stone was growing! Larger and larger it became, until an enormous swirl of black morphed into feathers, head, beak, claws. With a great cry, "Graa," its giant wings burst forth. The raven lifted off from Kane's paralyzed hands and flew directly above the meadow. Kane's men let out cries of fear as the great bird mocked them from above.

Kane's victory cry swelled into a great lingering shriek of rage, which drowned out the cries of his men and echoed beside the triumphant cry of the raven.

"Back to the village!" thundered Conall, as he grabbed Mia's hand and gestured his men to turn north. "Run!" We can defend from within the village! Gather all our men, all our arms," he called out in his great deep voice. "Get word to our allies and neighboring villages – we will crush the invaders!"

He turned to Liam, "Lead them," he said quietly.

With Liam in the lead, the Celts and the Native American men headed off through the woods, vanishing from sight and the twins, Patrick, Conall, and Mia followed at a distance.

However, once safely away from the meadow and out of sight of Kane and his men, Conall turned right, leading the small group off on a divergent path. He spoke quietly over his shoulder, "Make haste, my young friends, follow me."

Turning eastward with Mia at his side, he headed for Ninham Mountain, with the twins and Patrick hard on his heels.

———❦———

Chapter 22

———❖———

For the second time on this strange day, the twins were racing away from the meadow, but this time was very different. Unspoken tension and anxiety were in the air. With Mia leading the way, the group ran in loose formation, strung out in a line, winding their way through the trees, with Conall at the rear. Nadia knew Conall had placed himself intentionally between the twins and his brother Kane.

They had diverged from the beaten path, which served to make them less visible and harder to track. Mia navigated the landscape as if she were a woodland creature, not a human. Her feet landed unerringly on solid ground and she seemed to flow over obstacles. Even Patrick found it hard going to keep up with her. It was far more difficult for the twins and the effort was taking its toll. Nadia found she had to focus constantly just to keep from stumbling and Aidan was not faring much better.

Everything had happened so fast, Nadia was still trying to process it. Her brain kept replaying the image of the stone in Kane's hand writhing into a living raven and streaking into the sky. So magical, so awesome, she thought.

Aidan, who was running beside her now, said, "Wasn't that just awesome?" And once again, she knew they were on the same wavelength. She gave him a thumbs-up but saved her breath… and he grinned.

Patrick, just ahead of them, called back, between panting breaths, "Nadia, Aidan try to keep your minds clear. We have no idea the true extent of Kane's powers. He has the shield and even worse, he may be able to follow us by our thoughts."

Conall, from his position at the rear, added "Whatever powers he now holds, my brother will not be fooled for long. We must make the most of our head start. We must get you two away as quickly as possible."

Aidan called out to her, "Nadia, it's just as I thought, or hoped, anyway. We are headed back to the stone chamber!"

Nadia's heart sang. Since he had not handed over the Ravenstone, Conall *must* still have it, she thought. So, they were going home! Oh, how she longed to go home!

"Patrick is right; clear your mind," said Conall. "My brother is skilled at reading peoples' intentions, as you are, young Nadia."

Everyone is a mind reader in this place, she thought, feeling a warm connection to her new friends. Then she suddenly realized why Conall had not taken them into his confidence about the raven's shape-shifting trick. He couldn't let anyone know his plan. It all had to be terrifyingly real, in order that Kane not suspect the ruse. Clever, she thought.

As he strode northward along the woodland path, Kane slowed, then stopped. He forced himself to settle, to calm. Rage is a great motivator, he thought, but it can divert you, lead you astray. And it is not a plan. He needed a plan. He took long deep slow breaths and closed his eyes. The anger inside of him transformed into determination. He stood in the shadows of the ancient trees, while his men charged ahead of him, pursuing the Celts and Indians who raced back to their village. That's what he had soldiers for, he mused.

He turned and tilted his head from side to side, then lifted it slightly, almost as if sniffing the air. He grunted to himself. Then he hauled his shield up and around from where it hung over his back and held it flat in front of him. The black stones on the right side of the shield, on the eastern side, were glowing. So, the stone was nearby. And it was not in the village. His eyes narrowed and a small smile lifted the corners of his mouth. In one swift movement, he slipped the shield back over his shoulder and took off to the east at a fast run.

Nadia focused on placing her feet carefully through the wooded terrain, over rocks, under branches, through small streams, jumping decaying logs. Aidan was right in front of her and she could feel his exhaustion matching her own. It felt like they had been running for hours and her breath was ragged. She had a stitch in her side. No one was talking and the urgency to keep moving had not lessened.

Suddenly she caught her foot on a root and fell, landing hard on her hands and arms. She cried out in pain. Aidan grabbed her hand and pulled her to her feet as Patrick and Mia hurried to help her. She rubbed at her forearm, which was scratched and bleeding.

"I'm OK, I'm OK. Keep going." Although near tears from the pain and exhaustion, she took a step forward. '"Ow!" she wailed, "My ankle. Oh, no... "

Aidan took her arm as she tentatively took another step. "Lean on me. We have to keep going." She nodded and took a few tentative steps. "I'm going to slow everyone down!" Angrily she brushed a tear from her cheek. "Well, I'll just have to manage."

Aidan smiled at her, but she could see the strain on his face. "I'll help."

She leaned on her brother for the first few steps, until she felt she was recovering, somewhat. But, she simply couldn't move as quickly as before. Come on, Nadia, you have to, she thought. Mind over matter, as Mom says. But, I could kick myself for not seeing that root.

With the sudden sound of a cracking branch in the distance behind them, everyone's head turned in unison. Just a falling branch, Nadia hoped. No one said a word, but the alternative was terrifying. Kane.

There was no time to waste. Nadia and Aidan glanced at each other, then pushed ahead, doubling their speed. Nadia felt fear tearing through her. She gritted her teeth, intent on running through the pain, when she realized it was feeling a bit better. Was it her imagination? Or was fear masking the pain? If that sound was Kane's approach, he was close.

When at last they burst into the clearing in front of the stone chamber, Nadia almost burst into tears. She felt as if she were coming up from holding her breath under water. They had done it!

Conall urged them all toward the dark entrance to the chamber. Mia hurried to join them. "Patrick, you too, I want you all in the chamber for safety. Aidan and Nadia, no time for long goodbyes, my friends, here is the stone." He plunged his hand into the pouch in his tunic, but a flurry of movement and a metal clanging sound sent them all spinning to stare back at the wood line.

Kane, his massive sword held high, was charging toward them. As the blade sliced through the air, sunlight glinted off its steel surface, like sparkling shards of glass. The twins and Patrick froze in place.

Not Conall. In less time than it took to start breathing again, Conall had hurled himself toward his brother. Nadia's heart stopped and panic filled her. As Aidan pulled her back toward the chamber, away from danger, her mind raced. What should they do? What *could* they do?

Kane closed the final distance and with practiced skill, swung his blade down at an angle toward his brother's weak side. Conall sidestepped and intercepted the blade with his own. The swords met in an ear-splitting clang. Sparks flew as Kane's sword scraped up the length of the steel, to catch and hold at the hilt of Conall's.

The brothers, now mortal enemies, stood face to face, inches apart, calling on every ounce of their physical strength. The long moment of intense struggle finally ended as Conall whipped his sword down and around in a circle, tearing Kane's sword from his grasp. It flew off to land several feet away, with a clatter.

Conall stepped back, to allow Kane to retrieve his sword. Honor, thought Nadia, and nobility. But, in a sudden flash of understanding, she also realized that honor was only part of it. Conall found it almost impossible to kill his twin, his womb-mate. This was blood, family, and he would do everything in his power to save the situation without death to his only brother.

"Ah, always the honorable one." Kane grunted as he caught his breath. He moved as if to pick up his sword, but while ducking down, he pulled a dagger out of his boot. Hissing, "Fool," he leaped at Conall, who yanked his sword up just in time to deflect the blade, a split second before it drew blood. The dagger flew out of Kane's hand.

Conall no longer hesitated. The time for honor was passed, too much was at stake. He lunged at Kane, swinging his blade in a fearsome blow. But they had learned fighting skills together as children and trained against each other for years. As if he had seen it coming and perhaps he had, Kane threw himself to the ground, escaping the blade that would have taken off his head. He rolled toward his weapon and in one graceful move, was back on his feet, sword in hand, circling his foe.

The two men, panting, circled each other warily.

Kane lunged, Conall parried, Kane lunged, again, again, again. The repeated clanging of the swords was deafening, the speed of the fight frightening.

Nadia stood terrified and mesmerized. She heard gasps from Mia, who stood near them with her hands over her mouth. As for Aidan, he was clutching her hand so tightly it ached. This was a life or death struggle between two mighty warriors, both at least six feet tall, at the peak of their physical prowess. As identical twins, they could not be more evenly matched. The consequences of the wrong twin winning were unthinkable.

Now it was Conall's sword that went flying, his turn to drop to the ground in a roll. He just missed, by a millimeter, the mighty kick aimed at his head. He sprang to his feet, to spin back and face his brother, who lunged once more. The sword passed a hair's breadth from his face. He grabbed Kane's wrist and smashed it across his own knee until Kane's sword flew from his hand.

Kane pulled back enough to land one mighty punch to Conall's jaw, then threw himself bodily into a furious attack. All pretenses were dropped, all rules forsaken. As they rolled and wrestled and grappled in the earth, there was no other sound but the grunting desperation of the brothers. Nadia realized she could now no longer tell them apart, they were so covered in dust and blood.

Suddenly, in this to-the-death struggle, Kane had managed to regain his dagger and he slashed savagely across Conall's chest. Conall pulled back as far as he could.

It was not far enough.

The dagger's deadly point seared through his flesh and sliced through the straps to the Ravenstone's pouch. The black stone flew out and rolled to a stop ten feet away, glowing and pulsing, red and gold.

Blood pouring down his tunic, Conall staggered, but he lunged for Kane as his twin rushed toward the stone. Kane fought his brother off and threw him to the ground. Conall lay still and silent.

Nadia gasped. She hadn't even seen Patrick leave the safety of the chamber and rush to grab the stone. But, Kane had regained his footing and was closing the distance from the other side. When Patrick snatched the stone from the ground, Kane plowed into him like a charging bull. The Ravenstone flew from Patrick's hands as he hit the ground with a groan.

Kane whirled to claim his prize but screamed in anger. The raven had swooped across the clearing and now clutched the black stone in its claws. It winged toward the twins, dropped it in Aidan's hands and came to rest on the doorway of the stone chamber. The mighty bird's familiar "Graa" ended in a victorious shriek.

"Go!" shouted Patrick. "Aidan, Nadia, Go! Use it, go now."

Aidan hesitated for one second, looking at Conall's motionless body and Kane began to rush toward them.

Patrick screamed, "It's the stone he wants. If it's gone there's nothing to fight for. Take it, go!"

Quick as a flash, Nadia grabbed the other end of the Ravenstone and began to mutter, "The night we left, same time, same place." She locked eyes with Aidan, who continued the words like a mantra.

Suddenly there was the light, the golden arc, the cacophony of noise and the path drawing them forward. The clearing, Mia, Patrick, Conall, and Kane rushing toward them began to blur into a fuzzy haze.

As Nadia stared at the face of Kane hurtling toward her, she saw him leap through the air, arm outstretched, toward them. Oh no! His hand seized her sleeve. And his bloody face lurched into view. Nadia tried to punch at him with her free hand, but his grip was like a vice, his steel blue eyes boring into her. She hit him with all her might, again and again, but she could not pry him loose.

The unimaginable had happened: they had finally escaped the past but Kane was traveling with them.

"Aidan," Nadia shrieked, over the deafening sound.

At the same instant, she heard her brother's roar. He had grabbed the flashlight and it was now in his hand, aimed at Kane's face. He punched the button and beamed the full blinding light into Kane's staring eyes.

"Arrrrrgghh!" Kane screamed and let go, to clutch at his eyes, seared by the power of the beam.

Then he was sucked away, still shrieking, spinning and whirling into blackness, into the dark hole of time and space.

Chapter 23

———❖———

The bright arc of golden light faded, the roaring noise died away. The twins stood in the doorway of the stone chamber, clutching the stone. A shaft of silvery moonlight splashed across their feet.

Nadia let out a deep breath and waited for her head to stop spinning, to the adrenaline rush and fear of Kane would take longer to resolve. She was shaking.

"You OK?" he asked.

Nadia gazed around, getting her bearings, but turned to him and nodded. "Are we home?" Her voice trembled a little.

Aidan took a deep breath, reached for the flashlight, then stepped out beyond the chamber opening and swept the beam across the clearing. "Well, it sure isn't 459 – look, the altar and fire pit and everything is gone. Wait, we can check – the bikes!"

He hurried over to the clump of pines where they had hidden their bikes, with Nadia behind him, still limping a little from her injured ankle. There, lying exactly where the twins had left them, tucked out of sight, were their bikes.

Aidan reached into his helmet, grabbed his cell phone and punched the home button. The tiny screen sprang to life and the glow reflected off Aidan's face.

"Well Nadia, we did it. We're home. It's 3:02 in the morning – June 22nd, 2016."

Nadia was still trembling. She nodded. The relief was enormous, but oh, what about their friends?

Aidan said, "I know what you're thinking. Are they all right? I mean, what happened to them? Conall wasn't moving when we left. How will we ever know if he is all right?"

"I know we had to come home but I felt so bad leaving them in such danger," Nadia shook her head. "We put all their lives at risk. We brought all that disaster to them."

"Yeah, but we did get the Ravenstone away from Kane and we got rid of him, too! That counts for something doesn't it?"

She nodded, slowly, thinking hard. "I guess so, but where did he go? Is he dead?" She shuddered. "It was awful."

"I know. Maybe he landed in some other place and time. We'll never know. And I guess we will never know what became of Conall, of Patrick. Of Mia... "

The kids were quiet for a moment or two.

"Well, let's go home." Nadia reached down for her bike. "We have to get the plants to Dad."

"Wait a minute! Hang on, we can't go home yet!" Aidan turned back to the stone chamber. "Remember?"

"Wow, you're right!" She hurried after him.

She and Aidan had to use the Ravenstone; they had to time travel again. In their panic to get away from Kane, they had forgotten! If the Black Fern could save their dad's Project, they needed to get it to him while he still had his funding and had time to analyze the plant. They had decided on five years ago. Considering the dangers of going back in their own lives and possibly changing time in ways they could not imagine or undo, they had concluded that the risk was worth taking. They hoped. The plan was to arrive in 2011, in the dead of night and stay only the few brief minutes necessary to put the envelopes on their dad's desk. Then scoot back to current time.

Once back in the doorway of the stone chamber, Aidan held out the Ravenstone and waited for Nadia to take the other end. "OK. We focus on the attic, in front of the mirror. And let's get the plant envelopes out now, so we don't have to fumble around with them when we get there. I have no idea what would happen if we were to run into ourselves five years ago. We were eight. Yikes. Bad enough to run into Mom or Dad or Heather."

Nadia grimaced at the thought. "Absolutely. Hey, you still have the flashlight in your pocket? Going to need it – it'll be dark in the attic."

Aidan patted his pocket and nodded. "OK. We are going to the same night, same time but 2011."

"Got it," she replied, closing her eyes.

Together they focused and almost instantly the electric sensations began, then the huge arc of golden light, then the roaring sound. The stone chamber and the clearing faded away and they were swept along the now familiar golden path of time. They hung on tight. After several more moments, the swirling energy began to fade and they were in quiet darkness.

Nadia could just make out her reflection in the old cheval mirror. Then a beam of light hit the ground and she could see her brother, holding the flashlight in his other hand.

Aidan grinned and spoke softly. "Hey, gettin' good at this, doncha think?"

She nodded. It was definitely easier every time, Nadia thought.

Aidan gestured for her to follow, clicked the flashlight to its low beam and crept down the attic stairs. Nadia waited while he listened intently at the door – stumbling into themselves or their family was not an option! Aidan looked back at her, nodded and headed quietly down the hall.

Nadia stopped briefly outside her own bedroom door where she assumed her eight-year-old self was sleeping. She was sorely tempted to open the door and peek in at herself. Aidan grabbed her arm and shook his head, hard, his eyes wide. She shrugged her acknowledgment. He was right, what on earth was she thinking?

The twins scurried on, making no sound as they crept cautiously down the stairs. Geez, Nadia thought, we are getting pretty good at this sneaking around thing, too, she thought with a grin.

Then they slipped across the kitchen and into their father's office. Nadia placed the envelopes, which contained their hard-earned and priceless treasure, on his desk.

Just as they were turning to go, Nadia caught sight of something stuck to one of the envelopes. It had caught in the sticky adhesive of the flap. It was a feather from one of those beautiful pigeons that had come to their aid. She gently pulled open the flap, poked the feather inside with the samples of

Black Fern and firmly sealed it again. As she turned back to her brother, Nadia grinned at him and shrugged, proud of her little bit of mischief.

They made it back up to the attic in record time, without incident and took their place in front of the mirror.

"OK, one last time, we are really going home now," Nadia whispered.

"Yup. We can go back tomorrow and get our bikes. Let's just get home. Mirror again, OK?"

Nadia agreed. "Right. Here we go. 3 A.M, right here in front of the mirror, June 22nd, 2016."

A few moments of concentration and once again, the miracle happened. They floated through time and space in the familiar golden light, along the glowing pathway. Then it was over.

"We're home." Aidan peered down at his phone, which confirmed the time and date. "Phew," her brother said. "Let's be smart and put the Ravenstone where we know it's safe." He bent down, pressed the tiny button under the mirror and slid the black stone into the secret drawer. It closed with a soft click.

Aidan shook his head and sighed deeply. "I feel like I could sleep for a year."

"Home," Nadia said. "That was a really, really, long day."

Nadia slowly opened her eyes and blinked at her bedside clock... 5:45 A.M With the lingering fog of half-sleep tugging at her, for a brief moment she didn't know where she was.

Then it all flooded back to her. Everything that had happened: the Indian village, their new friends, the magical raven, the horrendous battle, the moment they left the wonderful plant on their father's desk.

She clambered over Nicky, who let out an indignant "Mroww!" Jumping up from the bed, she suddenly remembered something else: yesterday she had helped her mom in the arboretum to propagate more Black Fern plants. Wait, what? Arboretum? She peeked out the window as she grabbed her bathrobe and stopped to stare.

There, built onto the side of their house was a large glass-walled arboretum, like an elegant Victorian greenhouse or conservatory. Wow, she thought, Aidan has got to see this! She shot out of her door and slid to a stop at his. She tapped softly and peeked in. "Aidan!" she whispered.

He snapped awake, shook off the cobwebs and hurried out to join his sister in the hall.

"Come look at this!" Nadia dragged him by the arm to her window.

"What?" He pulled back in surprise as he saw the new glass extension. "Oh, wow."

"I know!" Nadia tried to keep her voice down, not wanting to wake her parents, but she could barely contain herself. "I think we've changed time. Things are definitely *different*!"

"Things... there is something else?"

"Yeah – it's even weirder. I *remember* stuff from yesterday – *here*, yesterday. I remember being in that arboretum with Mom, helping her plant new Black Fern cuttings. Aidan, before this minute I didn't even know what an arboretum was and now we have one! And I remember helping Mom and Dad design it! Come on." She scooted to the door.

Still in pajamas, he raced after her, slipping downstairs to the dining room. Where there had been a solid wall before, there were now French doors. Other changes caught Nadia's eye, but she didn't stop to process a different sofa here, a different rug there. Aidan unlocked the doors to the magnificent glass room and they quietly stepped down into a glorious plant heaven! Tables and tables and shelves and shelves of plants filled the space and the fragrance of the Black Ferns filled the room.

Nadia jumped up and down and whispered, "Awesome! But wait – this should all be new to me, but it isn't. You know what I mean?"

Aidan nodded and spoke slowly. "I remember it all, too. I remember Dad telling us about the new plant arriving on his desk. I remember how excited he was when the test results came through... how well it worked on antibiotic-resistant bacteria. It was the happiest I have ever seen him."

"Oh Aidan, he's nominated for the Nobel Prize in Medicine!"

Aidan gaped at her. There was a pause while they stared at each other. Then he nodded, slowly. "Dr. Michael Shaw, our dad... He is famous, now."

"How do we know this?" Nadia's brain was racing.

Aidan looked around him at the beautiful glass-walled room, with the hundreds of plants. He answered slowly, "We lived through those five years. We remember it because we lived it. But, we have the memories of the other five years, too. We have two sets of memories."

They locked eyes, then spoke at the same moment. "Let's go ask the old shaman in the mirror."

Chapter 24

As quietly as she could, Nadia raced after Aidan, up to the attic. All the while memories… new memories… of the last five years swirled around in her head. Memories of a different life that, until yesterday, she hadn't lived. How weird was that? Many things were the same, but there was a lot that was different! There was joy and celebration when the Black Fern was discovered to be a profoundly powerful healing plant. There was her father's new state-of-the-art laboratory. She was so proud that her brilliant father lectured to doctors and scientists the world over. I mean, seriously, The Nobel Prize in Medicine!

Although her dad's success had brought a new level of wealth to the family, it didn't really change much about her life. She still didn't get to buy something just because she wanted it, she thought with a grin. However, Aidan did get that great mountain bike he wanted for Christmas last year, something called a Yeti Enduro bike. That was cool. And, Mom had promised her a trip to England next year. She had wanted to see London for as long as she could remember.

But more importantly, she thought, having survived their bizarre and terrifying experience, she was just happy to be home… safe… with her parents and with her dad so happy. She felt herself misting up.

As they approached the old mirror, it happened again: Aidan said exactly what she had just been thinking.

"You know about the new bike they gave me?" When she nodded, he continued, "Well, it gets me wondering. What happened to the old one? Are our bikes still up on Ninham Mountain, by the stone chamber? Or are they *not* there because we changed time?"

Nadia thought for a moment. "That would mean... since we were living the lives where Dad *did* have the Black Fern, did we *not* find the stone? Or time-travel at all?"

"If we go with that... Then did we *not* find the Ravenstone because we didn't need to? But we *did* find the stone, that's how everything changed..." Aidan threw his hands in the air. "Oh, man, you could go nuts thinking about this."

Nadia remembered something else: the Passenger Pigeons. "And what about those cool birds – the extinct ones. Remember? The Passenger Pigeons?"

"Yeah, that was awesome! The birds that saved us! I can't believe all those birds are now gone. I looked them up; they were hunted to extinction over a hundred years ago."

She nodded. She was remembering that, at the time, no one could figure out how a feather from a bird, extinct since 1914, could turn up in an envelope on her father's desk. Her dad had sent it off to be identified and they had learned about the Passenger Pigeons. At the time, it hadn't meant much to her.

The twins shook off their memories, old and new and turned their attention to the stately old mirror. Awakened by their presence, their intention, and by the Ravenstone now tucked in the drawer underneath, the surface once again came to life. The glass shimmered and rolled as the image began to come into focus. There he was, the craggy old man in the familiar brown robe, wooden staff in hand. Nadia could not suppress a smile as the iridescent and ever-present raven cocked his head and met her eye.

The old man raised his hand in greeting. "Hail, my young friends. You have done very well."

Nadia was surprised at how much better he was able to speak to them.

Aidan said, "Thank you, sir. We have so many questions. And you are so clear this time!"

The old man nodded, slowly. "You are more receptive. The power of the Ravenstone has grown and imparted some of its power to you. You have both come a long way."

Nadia spoke. "Please, sir, tell us what happened to our friends. Conall, is he... was he all right? And Patrick and Mia?"

"Yes, although Conall was seriously wounded, he recovered, thanks to Mia's healing wisdom and the power of the Black Fern. He lived a long, full life, with his beloved Miakoda and their children. And he taught and guided Patrick who became a powerful healer and shaman, himself."

"Oh..." Nadia let out a sigh of joy and relief. She was so deeply grateful and thrilled their friends had fared so well. So odd, so sad, to think they are all dead, now and had been for centuries.

"Thank goodness," said Aidan. "And Kane? What happened to him?"

The old shaman's face became grave. "I will not speak of Kane. Best to leave evil where it lies."

Before the kids could ask more questions, the old man spoke again. "There is another request I must ask of you. Bring your Grandmother Elizabeth here to the mirror. She carries a great burden. It is time to ease her mind."

Aidan stammered, "Her burden? Grandma Liz? How can–

"You have trusted me with your lives. Now trust me again. This story is not yet complete. I need to speak with your Grandmother. Bring her to me." The image faded and they were once again alone in the attic.

Nadia turned to her brother. "The story is not complete? What does that mean? Uh-oh, what's going to happen when we see Aunty-Gran? Wasn't it just yesterday that she cornered us in the kitchen?" She grimaced. "She said she wasn't done talking about the stone... and she wasn't happy. Yikes. But wait, that was before..."

"Yeah, it's possible that now she doesn't know anything at all about us finding the stone," Aidan said. "Huh, it's so confusing, it makes my head hurt! We're going to have to be careful juggling two sets of memories."

Nadia suddenly saw the humor in the whole thing. She shook with laughter; hand over her mouth, not daring to laugh out loud. It was way too early to wake up their parents and before facing them she'd like a little time to get used to the new reality! "We're just going to have to wing it, aren't we?"

"Uh-huh. Guess so. In the meantime, Aunty-Gran said she was coming over to breakfast. I'm just not sure whether that was old Aunty-Gran or Aunty-Gran 2.0..." He screwed up his face like his brain was tied in a knot. This sent Nadia off into fits of giggles again, which soon had Aidan laughing as well.

"Shh! Keep it down!" Aidan shoved an old pillow over her face and she laughed even harder. She laughed so much she got the hiccups. She realized she was exhausted, relieved, and a bit overwhelmed, all at the same time.

It didn't take much persuading to get Grandma Liz to come up to the attic with them. They had dragged Grandma Catherine's old trunk, full of photos, old diaries, and dolls from her childhood, near to the cheval mirror. They just told Aunty-Gran they'd found something in the attic they wanted her to see and the older woman's eyes grew big. Nadia felt a wave of uneasiness coming from her grandmother, plus longing, and a touch of regret. She suspected Aunty-Gran must think, or hope, or fear that they had found the Ravenstone.

As she and Aidan stood near the mirror, the image of the wise old man quickly appeared.

"Aunty-Gran, look," said Nadia, gesturing toward the mirror and touching her grandmother's arm.

Looking up from the trunk, her grandmother caught sight of the old man, now fully formed as an image, in the mirror. She peered, turned slowly, and moved a little closer to study the old cheval.

"Hello, Elizabeth." As he spoke, the old man raised his hand to greet her and Nadia thought her grandmother might faint. Grandma Liz gasped and clasped her hands over her mouth.

Aidan said quickly, "It's OK, Aunty-Gran, he's a friend. You can trust him."

"What on earth... oh my... what's going on?" Grandma Liz cried.

Nadia reached out to her grandmother and stroked her arm, feeling helpless. She felt bad that her dear Aunty-Gran was so shocked. "Aunty-Gran, it's all right," she whispered. "Just listen to him. He has something to tell you."

"Elizabeth, you are not responsible for your sister Catherine's death." The old man spoke firmly and clearly.

Grandma Liz moaned.

The old man continued, "What happened to her was her destiny and she met it with exceptional grace."

Nadia's mind was racing. What? Aunty-Gran not responsible for her own sister's death? Destiny?

Before she could ask what he meant, the image of the shaman faded and another image morphed in his place. There stood an elegant, middle-aged woman who looked like a much younger Grandma Liz. She was dressed in a soft gray sweater and slacks with beautiful swept up hair and pearl earrings. This must be Grandma Catherine! Nadia thought.

Grandma Liz drew in a breath of shock.

"Hi, Liz." The woman in the mirror smiled and reached out her hand, as if hoping she could touch the twin sister she had not seen in 25 years.

Grandma Liz, her voice cracking and choked, stared at her sister. "Cathy? Oh, Cathy, is that you?"

"Liz, I don't have long. Listen, dear heart. You were *not* responsible. You have to let that go."

"Oh Cath, I'm so sorry, I'm so sorry. I tried so hard to find the stone, to see if I could go back to an earlier time before we found it... to tell us *not* to use it again... I am so sorry I coaxed you into making that trip to the future. If we hadn't done it..." Tears ran down her cheeks. "If we hadn't done it, you wouldn't have gotten sick..." Her voice trailed off into sobs. "You'd still be here," she wailed.

"Liz, wait. Liz. Listen to me. I am content with the way things turned out. This was my destiny, do you hear me? My *destiny*. My purpose in this life was to bring Michael into this world and set him on his path. Look at all he has achieved, Liz, all the people he has helped. I am so very proud of my son!"

Grandma Liz stood stunned, blinking back tears, taking that in.

Catherine continued quietly, "Michael's path was more important than my life."

There was a long, profound silence.

Then Grandma Catherine's image began to fade and she called out, "Be happy, my dear sister!" just as she vanished from sight.

The old man took her place. "We only have moments, the power is weakening. Be comforted, Elizabeth, giving up your life for the good of humankind is the greatest gift one can give. It is the greatest honor one can receive."

Tears were streaming down Grandma Liz's face and Nadia thought her heart would break. Aidan wrapped his arms around his grandmother and she wept on. After a long while, Grandma Liz took a deep shuddering breath and a small smile formed on her lips.

"Thank you both. So much. Thank you." She wiped her eyes. "May I lie down in your bedroom for awhile, Nadia?" She held her hand up and shook her head when the kids tried to help her downstairs. "I'll be OK, guys, I just need to be by myself for awhile."

As the attic door closed behind their grandmother, they turned back to the mirror.

"I have one last request, Nadia and Aidan Shaw." The old shaman spoke again.

Aidan perked up, "Do we get to time travel again? With the Ravenstone?

The shaman held up a hand. "You now know the Ravenstone carries great power and you have proven yourselves worthy stewards of that power."

"How can we help, sir?" Nadia spoke breathlessly, in anticipation.

"Travel to June 6, 1892. That was the day Nora was left abandoned in the doorway of the Ninham Mountain stone chamber."

The twins stood silently, listening.

Aidan nodded. "Then what?"

"Tell her that her brother is OK. That he was not lost. Tell her what you know of his life. That he was fulfilled in his path."

Chills ran up and down Nadia's spine, as the ghost of an idea crept into her mind. It couldn't be! Could it? She shivered. "Sir," she said, and her voice broke. "Who are you?"

"Why, my young friends, do you not know me yet? My name is Patrick."

The End

About the Authors

Diane Solomon enjoyed a wonderfully diverse career path that included her own variety show on BBC TV in England and major tours with Glen Campbell and Kenny Rogers. Her highly successful singing career has given way to her lifelong dream of being a writer.

This is the first novel written with her husband, Mark Carey, a retired biologist, naturalist, and accomplished voice-over artist.

They live in New Hampshire, on 55 acres of woods and streams, where they spend many hours designing gardens and meadows, and watching wildlife.

Website: www.EloquentRascals.com

Author's Note

Our apologies to Cold Spring and Ninham Mountain purists, who may realize that we have played fast and loose with geography in this book. Ninham Mountain is a bit further from Cold Spring than we have indicated. But, it served our purposes to tuck it nearer to the town, so we employed a wee bit of creative license!

Resources

Books about stone chambers and other mysterious phenomenon of the northeast:

Mysterious Stone Sites in the Hudson Valley of New York and northern New Jersey, by Linda Zimmermann

Celtic Mysteries of New England, Philip Imbrogno

The Stones of Time: Calendars, Sundials, and Stone Chambers of Ancient Ireland, by Martin Brennan

Websites:

The town of Cold Spring, New York:
www.ColdSpringLiving.com

America's Stonehenge. www.StonehengeUSA.com

Diane Solomon & Mark Carey: www.EloquentRascals.com

Made in the USA
Columbia, SC
17 June 2019